For Amy, who pushed me.
In memory of Kathleen Hinni

PROLOGUE

There was a knock at the door. Gwen stayed in her chair by the living room window, hoping that Percy, upstairs in his room, would hear and answer it. He didn't.

The knock came again, harder. Gwen pushed herself up and limped to the door, leaning on her cane. She opened the door.

There stood Molly, cheeks red, eyes blazing. Before Gwen could say a word, Molly took a step forward and pointed at Gwen's chest. "You ratted on me!"

"What?"

"You ratted me out! Called the cops and got me in trouble."

"I did not!"

"It must've been you. You're the only one who was close enough to see!"

"It wasn't me!"

"Who else could have –"

Gwen pointed back. "And what were you doing in the cabin, anyway?"

Molly ignored the question. "If it wasn't you, then how did they know?"

"I'm telling you, it wasn't me! I was in the hospital when it happened."

Molly paused. "The hospital? What for?"

"I was in an avalanche."

"Oh yeah, I heard about that." Molly's voice was softer now. "Heard your dad got banged up real bad."

Gwen stiffened. "Yes." She gripped the cane tighter.

Molly seemed to notice it for the first time. "You get hurt too?"

Tears stung Gwen's eyes. She would not cry in front of her former best friend. As if Molly cared, anyway. Gwen nodded. "My leg."

Molly didn't answer, watching Gwen with her piercing green eyes. "Well, someone squealed. And now I have to come every day and do work for your family, to make up for the cabin."

"Here?"

"Yeah."

"Every day?" Gwen asked.

"Yeah. And that sucks."

It does suck, Gwen thought. She said, "It's not my fault."

Instead of replying, Molly turned away.

Gwen closed the door, hobbled to the living room, and slumped in her chair. She stared, unseeing, at the horizon.

This was terrible. It was bad enough with her mother and Percy and her friends hovering over her . . . but Molly too?

How was she going to hide from Molly?

ONE: ONE WEEK EARLIER

Mrs. Truman clapped her hands. "All right, let's run it again. Positions, everybody."

Gwen took her place on the left side of the dance studio, facing the back wall, Carley to her right, Janelle behind her, the others gathered in a loose group.

"And five, six, seven, eight . . ." Mrs. Truman pressed play on the sound system, and the music started, a fast African drumbeat. Gwen took three steps back, then contracted her body, knees bent, lower back curved over, arms coming up in front, palms flat and pushing away.

"Contract – *unh!* – and release – *ahhh* . . . ," said Mrs. Truman. "Let's see those fingers spread, Janelle. Give it some oomph. And step back-side-front . . ."

A woman started singing, chanting words that Gwen didn't understand but that had a warm, celebratory feeling to them. Spinning around to the front, Gwen burst into a leap, arms raised.

"Step, step, prepare, and turn. That's an outward pirouette, Carley," said Mrs. Truman.

"Oops."

Mrs. Truman stopped the music and gave Carley an exasper-ated smile. "You know this, Carley. Step left, step right. Now you're ready for your pirouette, and the logical way to turn is . . . ?"

Giggling, Carley motioned to the left.

"Right," Mrs. Truman said. She turned to Janelle. "And, Janelle, on that expansion, I want to see strong arms and hands. Gwen, can you demonstrate?"

Gwen bent her knees, arched her chest, and stretched her arms to either side, spreading her fingers as far as they could go. She felt the inhale of breath, the opening out.

"Beautiful, Gwen. Everybody, look. In other places, the movement is loose and free, but here I want that moment of strength. Let's see it, Janelle."

Janelle bent her knees and opened her arms, her fingers loosely spread.

"More!" Mrs. Truman urged as Janelle stretched her hands wider. "More! That's it. Yes! Good. Feel that?"

Janelle nodded. Gwen knew it was hard for her. Years of ballet training had given Janelle beautiful technique but also a certain stiffness; she had trouble letting go. Gwen was the opposite, she thought ruefully; she had loads of passion but less-than-perfect technique.

"Thanks, Gwen."

Gwen came out of the release, blushing. It was flattering that Mrs. Truman often called on her to demonstrate. She just hoped the others didn't think she was showing off.

"Let's start again," Mrs. Truman said. She turned the music back on, and Gwen fell into the familiar movements. After a while, a male voice joined the female one, adding a layer of harmony, and the drumbeat got louder. Gwen let her upper body then fall to the right, then swing to the left, fingers brushing the floor. She lifted up and suspended at the top for a breath-held moment, then fell and swung in the opposite direction. She loved that feeling of falling, sinking, giving in to gravity. That was what African dancing was all about, the connection to the earth, the knees bent, the upper body loose and free.

They moved into another leap, and out of the corner of her eye, Gwen watched Carley soar. Her friend might be absent-minded, but she was built like a willow, all arms and legs. And when she leaped, she stayed airborne for what seemed like an impossible time. Gwen had once asked her how she did it, and Carley had shrugged. "I just think *up*," she'd said with a grin.

"Left arm. Right. *Oof!* Really punch it. That's it, Janelle, you got it. Head left, right, and step, step, and throw the arms."

They ran through the dance several more times. At the end of class, while the girls were mopping their faces and pulling on their jeans, Mrs. Truman called for attention.

"I have something exciting to tell you about," she said.

Gwen, taking a drink of water, capped her bottle and turned to face her teacher. Mrs. Truman was holding a sheaf of papers.

"The University of British Columbia Dance Department is

holding a special workshop for young dancers this summer, with an emphasis on choreography. It's called Dancemakers and it's for teens aged fourteen to eighteen."

Dancemakers.

A shiver went up Gwen's back.

Mrs. Truman held up the flyer. "It's a three-week program. There are daily technique classes and choreography workshops with leading choreographers. It finishes with a recital show-casing student-composed dances."

There was a buzz of voices. "Wow. . . . UBC. . . . Sounds amazing. . . . Think I could get in?"

Gwen clutched her water bottle, her heart pounding.

"Now, it *is* rather costly," Mrs. Truman went on, "and I know that's going to be a problem for some of you."

"How much?" Janelle asked.

"Seven hundred fifty."

Gwen gasped.

"Of course, that includes room and board and all your classes," Mrs. Truman added.

"Count me out," someone said.

"Like, that would be how many hours of babysitting?" another girl asked.

"Fourteen thousand," someone answered, and everyone laughed.

Gwen pushed the money out of her mind, concentrating on what Mrs. Truman was saying next.

"You have to audition to get in. Auditions are in Vancouver, or you can send a video of a dance you've choreographed. Three minutes max."

Three minutes, Gwen thought. Three minutes to show them you deserved to be there.

"The competition will be stiff," Mrs. Truman continued, walking around the room and handing out flyers. "But many of you, I think, have a good chance of getting in." Her eyes rested on Gwen for a moment before she moved on. "And I'll be happy to help you work on your dances."

Amid a buzz of excited chatter, the dancers left in twos and threes. As Gwen finished pulling on her sweatshirt and boots, Carley and Janelle came over.

"Three whole weeks of dancing!" Gwen said. "Can you imagine? Making up dances, dancing day and night . . ."

"Amazing," Carley said.

"Incredible," Janelle added.

"You going?" Carley asked them.

Janelle sighed. "I'd love to. But we're going to be away then. How about you guys?"

"I'd never get in," Carley said. "I could make up a dance, but then I'd never remember it."

Gwen laughed. "As long as you put lots of leaps into it, you'd be fine."

Wrapping her scarf around her neck, Janelle said, "A girl I know in Kelowna went last year, and she said it was fabulous.

Killer classes, all-day rehearsals, but a great time. They stayed in a dorm and had a blast. And her dancing really improved."

Gwen imagined it. She saw herself in a studio, the wall of mirrors, the windows, the space. Feeling high on exhaustion and covered in sweat. Getting critiqued by professionals. Piling a throng of girls into someone's dorm room and chatting half the night.

"I'd kill to go," Gwen said, and her friends laughed. *But I really mean it,* she thought.

Carley and Janelle waved good-bye and left as Gwen buttoned her jacket.

"Gwen?"

She turned.

"What do you think?" Mrs. Truman asked.

Gwen's hands flew to her chest. "Oh, Mrs. Truman."

"You'd have an excellent chance. I'm sure of it."

"I've got to go."

"You'll make the age cutoff, won't you?"

Gwen nodded. "I'll be fourteen in June."

"Skin of your teeth," Mrs. Truman said.

Gwen giggled. Then she grew serious. "It's so much money."

"I know. I can't offer to pay your way, Gwen, but anything else I can do, I'm here."

"Help me with my dance?"

"Of course."

"Thanks!"

Gwen tucked the flyer in her dance bag and left. Outside, she was surprised to see that it was snowing lightly. It had been raining when she went into class. But this was one of those crazy winters. Normally it only rained in Thor Falls, about sixty miles up the coast from Vancouver. Endless storms through November, December, January, February, winds pushing clouds off the Pacific, colliding with mountains, dumping one rainstorm after another on the coast.

But not this winter. This year, some freaky weather thing was happening. They'd already had several dumps of snow, and here it was, early March, spring break about to start, and more was coming down. Bizarre.

Gwen stood a moment, watching the delicate flakes fall through the beam of light cast by one of Thor Falls' few street-lights, in front of the post office–slash–grocery store–slash–liquor store. Then she turned down the side road toward home, her dance bag slung over her shoulder.

Already she had a sense of the dance she wanted to create for the audition. Not the steps – not yet – but the feeling, the image. It would be a dance about her town, her mountain, her water-fall. A dance about water emerging from springs on the jagged peak of Mount Odin: trickles at first, merging into streams, gathering, widening, thundering over the ledge, crashing on the beach below – the roar that had been the musical accompani-ment to Gwen's life.

She stopped walking and listened. Yes, there it was. The noise of Thor Falls was muffled by the snow, but it was still there, constant and strong.

Without realizing it, Gwen thrust an arm upward as if she herself was the sheer granite face of the mountain that towered over the town. Then she smiled sheepishly, catching herself. Dancing in the snow. Nutso. Still, she quickened her pace, eager to get home and try out some ideas in her room.

How was she going to convince her parents? That was going to be the stumbling block. For starters, they never had any money. Her dad, Andrew, worked summers as a guide in Mount Odin Provincial Park, and her mom, Bridget, drove the school bus. They got by. Just.

And would they let her go by herself to Vancouver for three weeks? They'd say she was too young. At least her mother would. She always said *no*, no matter what the issue was. That was her initial position; why something was a bad idea. Her father was a little more glass-half-full. A little more on Gwen's side. So it would be better to start with him. She'd get him to agree, and then together they'd convince her mother.

She hoped. This was no sure thing, not even with him.

With a sigh, Gwen reflected that even just several months before, she would have run straight to her best friend, Molly, with this news. Molly would have whooped and hugged her and said it was fantastic, and then they would have put their heads together and figured out how to get her parents to say *yes*.

That was then. There was no running to Molly now. Gwen would have to figure it out by herself.

She would, Gwen vowed, skirting around the old cabin her parents had built when they'd first come to Thor Falls, before they'd built their current house on another part of the property, on a bluff overlooking the ocean. Sighting the warm yellow light spilling from the house windows, she began to leap through the snow.

Dancemakers.

She'd find a way. She had to.

TWO

I take another pull on my beer and let out a huge belch. That makes me grin. Leaning toward Nikki, I say, "Want to hear something amazing?"

"Sure, Molly. What?"

"Beer makes me burp!" This is something I've just discovered. Not that I haven't drunk beer before. But never so much at once. To prove the point, I take another gulp and burp again. "See?"

Nikki rolls her eyes. "Molly, that is freaking incredible."

I know she's slagging me, but it strikes me as hilarious and I burst out laughing.

"What's so funny?" Crystal yells over the music. She's sitting cross-legged in front of the gas fireplace, stoned as usual, watching the fake flames do their flickering dance.

"Nothing, Crystal," Nikki says. "Just Molly being drunk."

"I am not drunk," I say, wagging my finger. I burp again. "Oops. Yes, I am."

"Oh," Crystal says, still staring at the fire. She holds up her hands, palms facing the flames. "You know what? This fire's hot."

"No kidding, Crystal," Tony says, and everybody laughs.

We're in Nikki and Zach's living room. Their mom's out on a date, so we've gathered here tonight. It's the first night of spring break, a good excuse for a party. Although with these guys, I've found any excuse will do. Nikki and I are sitting on the floor, leaning back against the couch; Zach's sprawled in the easy chair, legs outstretched, with Gretchen sitting on one of the arms, playing with the brown hair curling over his neck; Tony's lounging at the other end of the couch. There's a bunch of empty beer cans on the coffee table, a roach in the ashtray, and Death By Juice's "Brain Dead" wailing through the speakers.

"Who's ready for another puff?" Tony asks, pulling a ziplock bag out of his pocket. I've noticed that he's the keeper of the dope. Also the guy who scores it. He lives in Norse River, where our high school is, and knows a guy with a grow-op in the woods. Good friend to have.

"Me!" Crystal says. A smile spreads across her face. She's such a stoner, with her blonde dreads and hemp pants and peace-sign necklace. Tonight she's got beads in her hair, and they click as she whips her head around, clickety-click — a chain reaction of bead collisions as the dreads swing one way — then clickety-click as they swing back. Crystal's like the original hippie chick. To be honest, I don't know why she hangs with this crew. From what I've seen, she hardly ever drinks, only downing a beer once in a while to take the edge off her mushroom trip or whatever other psychedelic she's on.

Tony rolls and lights the joint, takes a couple of tokes, and passes it to Crystal, who inhales deeply and hands it on to me with a blissed-out smile.

I take a toke, hold it in. Mercifully, I'm past the point where I choke every time – *that* was embarrassing. Aah. . . . The buzz hits in a minute. Between the beer and the pot, I'm feeling great. A little dizzy, but good-dizzy. Happy.

Death By Juice's lead guitar player goes into a thrashing solo, and Tony stomps his foot in rhythm. "Dig that," he says. "Are they the greatest metal band of all time or what?"

No way, I think. But before I can say anything, Zach shouts, "Hell, no!" He sits up suddenly, nearly dumping Gretchen off the arm of the chair. I snort, and she gives me a dirty look.

"No? Then who?"

"Rat's Nest."

"Yeah!" I shout, jumping to my feet and high-fiving Zach. "Annie Fresh is the best." I want to *be* Annie Fresh when I grow up. Of course I don't say that.

"You tell him, girl," Zach says, flashing me a smile. My heart does a flip.

"Are you out of your freakin' minds?" Tony says. "Rat's Nest doesn't even lick Death By Juice's boots."

I ignore that. Spreading my feet the way Annie Fresh does, playing an imaginary guitar low on my hips, picturing myself in knee-high, laced-up, high-heeled boots, a torn undershirt falling off one shoulder, I sing:

You are mine, all the time,
You are mine, I'm drawin' the line.
This love's just a ragged scar,
I can't feel where you are . . .

"Yeah!" Zach yells. He nods at me appreciatively. "Hey, you got a voice on you."

My cheeks feel warm. "Thanks." Suddenly shy and glad they don't think I'm weird, I sit down again. I haven't done this sort of thing – sing for people – since I used to sing for Gwen when we were kids. I'd try out little tunes I'd made up, sing my favorite songs from the radio.

As if it were yesterday, I remember this one time when she and I were playing in her old cabin. I'd made up a song about the Lady Who Lives in the Clouds, who causes all the rain and thunder and lightning. As I sang, Gwen danced, taking tiny, pattering steps for the rain, stomping her feet on the old floorboards for the thunder, and leaping to show the sizzling lightning.

I came to the end of the song. Gwen took my hands and sat me down across from her on the floor. "When we're grown-ups, you'll come to all my shows, and I'll buy all your records."

"What records?"

"You're going to be a famous singer, you know."

"I am?" I said stupidly.

"Of course!"

A flush spread from my belly to my face, and I gave a delicious shiver.

Now, I come back to myself. Famous singer? Yeah, right. Still, it's nice that someone likes my voice.

Tony flaps a hand. "You guys are wacko. Nothing can touch this band." He crosses the room and cranks up the volume. "Just listen." The drumbeat pounds through the floor. The lead singer's voice is a screech of defiance.

I nod my head in rhythm. They're good, all right. Just not as good as —

There's a banging on the door. No one moves. Again, louder. A woman's voice yells, "You kids turn it down in there or I'll call the cops!"

We hear her footsteps retreat from the front door. Everyone exchanges alarmed looks. Nikki goes over to the stereo and turns it down. "That Mrs. Allen is such a pain in the ass," she says to her brother.

"No kidding."

"You think she'd do it?"

"Nah," he says, cracking another beer.

Nikki looks uncertain. "We better cool it for a while, anyway. If she tells Mom, we won't be able to have anybody over."

"Bummer," Crystal says.

Gretchen nods. "We need another place to hang out."

"Where we can really crank it up," Tony adds.

And then it comes to me. Gwen's old cabin. Nobody uses it anymore, and it's far enough away from Gwen's house on one side, and the neighbors' house on the other, that no one would hear a party going on. At least, I don't *think* they would, anyway.

I gulp, thinking about the first time Gwen brought me there. We were little, five or six, and already best friends. As soon as we walked inside, I got a whiff of the dry, musty smell of the old wooden floors, the cedary aroma of the log stump chairs.

"This used to be my parents' house," Gwen told me. "I was a baby here."

She showed me the spot where her mom had rocked her in a cradle, the hook where the propane lantern had hung from the ceiling, the old woodstove where her parents had cooked their meals and heated their tiny house.

"Now it'll be our special place, okay?"

Okay? It was heaven. Room to play, tell secrets, laugh, make up stories. Space for Gwen to dance and me to sing. Just the two of us.

That day we swiped a knife from Gwen's kitchen and carefully carved our initials into the wall, down low in one corner. "G + M 4 ever."

I can still remember how we ran our fingers over the carving, staring into each other's eyes.

Now, I hesitate, wondering if I should tell them about the cabin. It's Gwen's. And it was our secret place.

Then I push the doubt aside. That old vow – "G + M 4 ever" – is broken, anyway.

"I know a place," I say, and everyone turns to me.

I tell them about the cabin. Smiles all around.

"Sweet," Zach says.

"Perfect," Tony says, giving me a thumbs-up.

I tingle. I haven't been hanging out with these guys that long. I got close to Nikki last summer, and she introduced me to the others when we started high school in the fall. Until now I haven't been sure if I belonged. Tonight I feel like I do.

"You got anything to eat?" Crystal asks out of the blue. "I got the munchies."

"You've always got the munchies, Crystal," Zach says, laughing.

Nikki finds some microwave popcorn and in a few minutes we're stuffing handfuls into our mouths. Gretchen, sickeningly, starts feeding Zach, kernel by kernel, as if he's her little baby. And then Nikki starts tossing pieces for Tony to catch in his mouth, and soon popcorn is flying everywhere and I'm laughing so hard it hurts.

As I whip my head to one side to catch a piece, I glimpse a clock. *Crap.* An hour and a half past my curfew. I'm really going to get it this time.

"Got to go, guys," I say, rooting around on the floor amid

the popcorn and empty beer cans for my hoodie. "See you."

Everyone calls good-bye as I stumble out the front door and down the walk. Whoa, it's snowing. Weird. I pull up my hood.

I stuff gum into my mouth, even though I know it's in vain. I probably smell like a brewery and reek of weed. And my dad is no doubt waiting up for me in the living room, one eye on the clock and the other on some TV show that he's not watching, rehearsing the speech he's going to give me about what a disgrace I am, how I'm so disobedient and disrespectful, and what a poor example I'm setting for my sisters. *What happened to the sweet girl you used to be?* he'll want to know. *You're grounded, young lady,* he'll say, *and get up to your room this instant.*

So what's new? Seems like I've spent most of the last year being yelled at, sent to my room, grounded.

Oh well, I think, walking past the dance studio on the main street of town. At least I had fun tonight. I focus instead on the tangy taste of the beer and the flying popcorn. I picture Zach's nod when I sang like Annie Fresh and the smiles on everyone's faces when I told them about the cabin. That's what I hold close as I walk through the snowy streets to my punishment.

THREE

The crinkle of paper woke Gwen up. Loud and crackly, it sounded as if someone was crumpling a sheet right next to her ear.

She felt beneath her cheek and knew, without opening her eyes, what was making the sound. The Dancemakers flyer. She must have fallen asleep holding it.

She sat up, flattening out the wrinkles against her chest, then glanced at her watch. Five o'clock. Still dark, but not completely. Something luminous in the dark, a silvery glow from outside.

Wrapping her quilt around her, she went to the window. Wow! It had really snowed. Smooth, unbroken white covered the yard, each fence post sported a curved cap, and the bed of her dad's pickup was filling with a cargo of snow.

Snow-bright light fell on the flyer in her hand, just enough to illuminate the title. She hadn't said anything about Dancemakers to her father last night. He'd been busy making dinner, then playing with Percy, so she hadn't managed to get him alone. She had to get her parents' permission and send in the form – and soon – so she could concentrate on her piece for the audition.

Her dance. The thrusting arm movement that she'd done last night in the snow came back to her. Tossing her quilt back on her bed, she rolled up her rug and pushed it aside. She raised her arm again, then slowly uncurled the other one until it too reached for the ceiling. Letting her head float up, she looked up, up, past her stretched fingertips. She rose onto her toes, taller, higher, then swept her arms down and across her body to the left, following them into a turn, circling her left leg in a fan kick, tracing a curve that echoed the surge of Thor Falls over the ledge.

The fan kick flowed into a contraction, knees bent, elbows tucked in, back curled over. Gwen exploded out of it into a jump, feet pointed down, arms upflung. Yes, the jump felt right. The lift, the length, the vertical line.

She stepped into an arabesque, leg lifted behind, arms in fourth position. No, that was too pretty, too balletic, she decided, looking in her dresser mirror. Something Janelle would do. Nothing wrong with it, but it wasn't right for this dance. Thor Falls was all about power, and her dance had to capture that raw force. The crashing spray, the wall of water, the vertical drop.

She drew her leg into her body, knee bent, then pushed it back behind her, foot flexed as if kicking something away, arms shooting forward. Yeah, *that* was the feeling she wanted. Percussion. Strength.

The dance was going to be good. She could feel it. She was discovering the movements, big and bold, the feeling of earth and water and stone. She'd find just the right music, saxophone and drums and electric guitar. And she'd get in.

Oh, please, she thought, pausing in her movements and snatching up the flyer again. *Please, please, please,* she prayed, not knowing who she was praying to – God or her dad or the people who would judge the auditions or the muse of dance itself.

Ten minutes later, the basics of the dance in place, Gwen headed downstairs. It was ridiculous to be up so early the first morning of spring break, but she was too wired now to go back to sleep.

She came through the kitchen door.

"Dad! What are you doing up?"

"What are *you?*"

They grinned at each other across the kitchen, her father, a short, stocky, red-bearded man in a flannel shirt and jeans, cradling a steaming mug in his hands; Gwen, slender and wiry, her hair in tangles from sleep.

"Couldn't sleep," they both said at once, and laughed.

"The snow, I guess," her father added, sipping coffee. "Too quiet. You know how it's so quiet you can hear it?"

Gwen nodded, thinking how they often shared the same thoughts, how it was so much easier to get along with him than with her mom.

Well, here he was. She touched the flyer in her bathrobe pocket for luck. "Um, Dad —"

"Gwennie, let's go up Odin!"

"What?"

"Let's ski on Odin. The snow'll be great. You want to?"

"Sure!" she said. The whole family had taken up telemark skiing recently, but she and her dad were the craziest about it; they loved skiing up rugged switchbacks and then soaring down. Usually they had to travel to find snow, but not this year. "When do you want to go?"

"Now!"

"Dad, it's five-thirty in the morning."

He waved his hand. "By the time we get there, it'll be light. I want to get on the mountain early. It's supposed to warm up later. I want to ski that powder before it turns to slop."

"Okay. What about Mom and Percy?"

"Let 'em sleep." He put an arm around Gwen's shoulder. "It'll be our adventure."

"Father-daughter bonding time," Gwen said drily.

He laughed. And Gwen realized this was perfect. She'd wait till they got up on the mountain. He'd be in a great mood. He'd agree to anything.

Gwen and her dad climbed out of the truck at the first bench. The snow was half a foot deep here, though Gwen knew it would be deeper up higher. It had stopped snowing for now, but the dampness in the air hinted that there was more to come.

Gwen fastened her cable bindings around her ski boots and slung her pack on her back.

"Here." Her father handed her an avalanche beeper, a small orange contraption about the size of a cell phone; it hung from a leather strap.

"There's not *that* much snow, Dad."

"Enough."

Gwen rolled her eyes. "You've been watching too many action movies, Dad."

"Put it on."

"Okay, okay." She hung the strap around her neck.

"Now make sure it's turned to *transmit*."

Gwen looked down. The words *transmit* and *receive* were printed on top. A little arrow pointed to *transmit*. "It is."

"Okay. Now, don't turn it off."

"I wouldn't dream of it, Daddy. An avalanche might come down and bury me."

"That'd shut you up, at least."

Gwen giggled. "I'll break trail," she said, grabbing her poles.

"You will?" Usually he did.

"I've got energy today."

The road climbed for a ways, then leveled out. The snow was slushier than she'd expected, so each stride was work. But her muscles felt good, and the reward, she knew, would come later, on the downhill ride.

At first, Thor Falls was out of sight around a curve. Then Gwen rounded the bend, and there it was: an endless stream of water like an upended river, churning over the ledge, arching outward and down, down, down. To her right, beyond the beach, the ocean glinted gray under a cloudy sky.

Gwen skied to the middle of the trestle bridge that crossed above the falls. Here the noise was so loud she felt as though she'd dived into an ocean of sound. She could feel the force of the water through the wooden beams of the bridge. Her whole body vibrated, and she suddenly felt unsteady, afraid she might topple over and be swept away by the surging stream.

Quickly she skied off the bridge, onto solid ground, then immediately felt silly. Swept away by Thor Falls. Yeah, right.

Her dad skied up behind her, pulled off his hat. His hair was curly with sweat. "Skis sticking?" he yelled above the water's roar.

She shook her head.

"Mine are." He tapped the bottom of one ski with his pole. "Seems to be getting warmer."

Now that he mentioned it, Gwen realized that she did feel warm. She unzipped her jacket, drank from her water bottle, offered it to her dad. He drank, then gave it back to her with a smile.

Now, while he's in a good mood, she thought. Then, *No, it was too noisy here. Better wait till we get away from the falls.*

"I'll break trail," her father shouted, and he went ahead.

Gwen followed, grateful for his tracks to glide in. He skied around a switchback and disappeared up the next ridge. When she came around the curve, he was standing on a ledge above the bridge, his skis and poles sticking up out of the snow. She skied up beside him, glad for the rest.

"Dad —" she started, but he plopped down on the snow. "What are you doing?"

"Eating," he said, unzipping his pack. "Here. I made sandwiches." He handed her one.

"But Dad —"

"Sit down, Gwen. You need energy."

"I know, but —"

"But nothing. Eat."

Gwen took off her skis and sat beside him. Mmm . . . peanut butter and honey on his homemade bread. She hadn't realized she was hungry. Well, as soon as they'd eaten, she'd tell him. Ask him. Beg him.

They ate in silence, watching the ocean waves roll in, listening to the plop of snow as the cedar boughs shed their loads. After a while, Gwen felt a few flakes on her face and realized it had begun to snow lightly. She glanced at her father. Good: he was finished. They put their skis back on.

"Daddy —"

"Sh."

"What?"

He cocked his head, listening for something.

"I don't hear –"

But then she did. A rumbling noise coming from below. She looked, but she could see nothing. The noise drew nearer, grew louder, more like a whining drone. Gwen glimpsed a flash of silver through the trees below. The drone rumbled louder, then a snowmobile sped around the switchback and pulled up behind them. The engine died and there was sudden silence again.

"Hey, Simon," Gwen and her dad said together.

Simon and his wife, Sally, were Gwen's parents' closest friends and an honorary aunt and uncle to Gwen and Percy. They lived on the property next to Gwen's family and were the first people her parents had met when, greenhorns from the city, they'd moved to Thor Falls. They'd helped Andrew and Bridget build the old cabin, showed them how to garden, how to dry blueberries for winter desserts, how to find the juiciest clams on the beach. Gwen often babysat their three young kids.

"Andrew, Gwennie," Simon said. He lifted his goggles and wiped the damp, black hair from his forehead with a sleeve. "How's the skiing?"

"Sticky. Seems to be warming up."

"Yeah, it's been heavy going," Simon said.

"So get out and ski."

"Too much work," Simon said, and they all laughed.

"How're the boys?" Gwen asked. Paul, Simon's older son, had caught the chicken pox in his kindergarten class and, after a miserable week, passed it on to his little brother, Jasper.

Simon rolled his eyes. "Paul's pretty much done, just a few scabs left, but Jasper's driving us nuts. Keeping us up half the night. To tell the truth, I don't think he's itching so bad, he just loves the attention." Gwen and her dad laughed. "At least Tanya seems to be spared. She's got that baby immunity."

Gwen smiled, thinking of Tanya. Her black baby hair stuck straight up in the air, and her eyes were like two shiny black pebbles.

A gust of wind blew a swirl of snowflakes around them.

"Getting thicker," Simon said.

"I know," Gwen's father agreed, a note of uneasiness in his voice.

Gwen noticed that it was snowing more heavily. What had, just a few minutes ago, been a light sprinkling was now a swirl of wet flakes that melted as soon as they touched your face. The ocean had disappeared behind a wall of white.

"I wouldn't stay up too long," Simon said.

"We're not," Gwen's dad said.

Simon turned the key and the snowmobile roared back to life. Smelly blue fumes clouded up around them. He waved, then droned on up the trail.

Gwen brushed the melting snow off her face. Now was her chance. "Dad —"

"We really should start heading down," he said.

"But —"

"Simon's right. Snow conditions are changing —"

"Dad, would you listen!"

He turned to her with a surprised look.

Suddenly she had no words to say. She reached into her pack and thrust the Dancemakers flyer into his hands.

"What's this?"

"Read it."

As his eyes scanned the paper, she waited to see his enthusiastic smile. But when he looked back up at Gwen, there was only a frown.

"Can I go?"

"You know we don't have that kind of money, Gwen."

That wasn't what he was supposed to say. "I know, but . . . I'll get it."

"You will? How?"

Gwen thought wildly. "I don't know. Babysit. Mow lawns. Walk dogs. It doesn't matter, I will somehow –"

He shook his head. "You'll never raise enough. And Mom and I just can't make up the difference."

"But –"

"And it's three weeks alone in the city. You're just a kid, Gwen."

"I am not! I'll be fourteen by then. I can take care of myself."

He shook his head again. "You don't know city life, Gwen. It's not like Thor Falls. There's crime. It's dangerous."

"I'm not going to be walking the streets alone at night!"

He patted her shoulder. "Wait a year or two. You'll be older.

Maybe we'll have more money –"

"There *is* no next year! It's now! It may never come again. Oh, Daddy, I've got to go, don't you see?"

He didn't answer.

Gwen felt everything going wrong. Desperately, she asked, "Can I go – yes or no?"

"Let's go down, Gwen," he said gently. "I don't like the look of this snow. We'll talk about it at home."

She planted her feet. "Yes or no."

"I can't say, Gwen. I've got to talk it over with Mom."

"Oh, great. She'll say no, of course."

"You're being unfair. Mom's not –"

"Unfair? You're the one who's being unfair!"

"Gwen, try and understand –"

"I understand, all right. You don't care about me –"

"Gwen –"

"Or what I want –"

"Gwen –"

"Or that I'll die if I don't go –"

"Gwennie –"

"I hate you!" Snatching the flyer from his hand and thrusting it into her jacket pocket, she turned away, dug her poles into the deep snow, and pushed off.

"Gwen, where are you going?"

She didn't answer. Didn't know. Just away. Her dream was dead. She skied away, uphill.

"Gwen, come back! We've got to go down."

"No!" She forced her skis through the wet, heavy snow. Her thigh muscles burned.

"Gwen, get back here!"

She ignored him, pushing herself harder, gulping deep breaths of air. The light was strangely flat; everything seemed to merge into a blur, and it was hard to see the path. She didn't care. She pushed on.

She became aware of a noise, a rumbling sound. She stopped and listened. Thor Falls? No, it seemed to be coming from above, not below. The noise got louder, closer. Was it the snowmobile? She looked around for Simon. No sign of him.

Louder now, roaring. Then a wind from high on the mountain, a wall of air that slammed against her.

"Ski, Gwen!" her father shouted from behind her.

Gwen stood there, not understanding. How could she ski with this wind pushing at her so hard that she had to struggle even to stand?

"Ski!" His voice was nearly lost in the roar that now was as loud as if they'd been standing right under Thor Falls.

Then she saw. Above her the mountain was moving. A wall of snow was tumbling downward, toward her. A fine layer floated above the churning mass, like a swirling cloud of flour. Beneath, white mounds tumbled over and over, gaining speed.

I'm going to die, she thought, frozen.

She made her legs move. Half-carried by the cold blast of air, she skied forward, slid off the trail, down the mountain. Propelled by wind and terror, she looked over her shoulder. The wall of snow was closer now, sliding unchecked. It was nearly on her father.

"Daddy!" she shrieked.

She lurched forward. Off to her right, she glimpsed the snowmobile speeding down the mountainside. The snow came closer now, rolling, roaring. It picked her up like a leaf and tossed her down. Her body twisted. She felt pain. The air whooshed out of her chest as the ground lurched up. Snow crushed her. Just before she lost consciousness, she saw her father's body flung several meters down the slope, then disappear under the roiling fury of snow.

FOUR

Two nights later, I'm walking down the trail to the Torrances' cabin, the others following behind. I've snuck out of the house, warning my sisters, on pain of death, not to tattle. Behind me, Zach is shining a flashlight to light my path, but I don't need it. The patches of snow – what's left after two days of rain – are bright. Besides, I've walked down this trail so many times my feet know the way.

As we get closer, I feel a pang. It feels wrong to be sneaking behind Bridget and Andrew's backs to use the cabin. I spent so much time at their house – it was so much more fun to play there than at my house, with my strict parents and annoying twin sisters – that I practically lived there. Bridget and Andrew fed me, patched up my scrapes, even scolded me when I was naughty – as if I was one of their own kids.

I almost hope the cabin will be locked.

But not really. We're going to have fun. And these guys are counting on me.

I come to the end of the trail where it meets the bluff, then turn right toward the small clearing where the cabin sits. A tall hemlock looms in the dark, blacker than the night. The brush has grown up so much, even in the year or so since I've been here, that I have to push through saplings to get to the door.

It's not locked.

I push it open and step in. It's cold and smells musty, but everything is just the same. The three stump chairs – for Gwen and me, and Percy when we let him play with us; the table made from a cable spool turned on end; a broken-down chair, one of Andrew's early carpentry efforts; a shelf with a few mugs and a kerosene lantern; the old woodstove.

I go straight to the spot where Gwen and I carved our initials. It's dark, so I have to feel with my fingertips, like we did that day. Sure enough, they're still there. I can feel the shapes of the letters, the angular *G,* the crooked number *4.*

I remember how Gwen and I hung a picture over the carving so her parents wouldn't know we'd used a knife. One day Andrew came to check on us. "What's that picture doing way down there?" he asked, pointing. "You should hang it up here, where people can see it."

He went to pull it off the wall, but Gwen stopped him. "No, Daddy, we want it down low, so . . . so . . ."

"So we can look at it when we're lying on the floor!" I finished.

Giving us an odd look, Andrew left. Gwen and I turned to face each other and laughed out loud.

Now, I shake myself back to reality as my friends crowd into the cabin. Gretchen lights a couple of candles – I've told them there's no electricity – and they look around.

"Wow!" Crystal says. "This is awesome."

"What a find," Nikki says. "Way to go, Moll."

I grin, glad they like it. The hell with memories. "Let's party!" I say.

Everybody deposits their booty on the table. Zach's scored a couple mickeys of vodka, Tony's got the pot, Nikki and Crystal have brought chips and chocolate bars for the munchies, and Gretchen's dug up a battery-powered ghetto blaster, a huge relic from her parents' basement, which she sets up on the shelf. She pops in a CD, and the opening bass notes of "U-R Mine" start laying down the beat. Zach and I high-five each other – Rat's Nest rules! – and soon Annie's voice, now trilling, now growling, fills the air.

Zach opens one of the bottles and we pass it around for a while. I don't tell them, but I've never drunk vodka before. It burns with a dry, rasping heat and I choke a little – but boy, it hits fast. In moments, I feel a warmth in my belly and that floaty, dizzy buzz in my head. Aah. . . . Next time, I don't choke. Or the next.

I start dancing as Rat's Nest goes into "Black Snow." Waving my arms overhead, I sing along, "Black snow, color of your soul, dirty secrets, out of control . . ." Stomping my feet, I grab the bottle as it comes by again. I wish Zach would dance with me, but Gretchen's pulled him down onto the floor and is making out with him. Oh well, I think, taking a hit from the joint that Nikki hands me. Zach's anchored. Bound and gagged. Gretchified. I laugh at my brilliant joke and dance even more wildly.

As I whirl around, I see that Crystal, who this time has stuck cedar fronds in her dreads so she looks like a stoned-out mermaid, has joined me. Only she's not dancing to Rat's Nest's beat, she's slowly swaying back and forth and rippling her arms like a piece of seaweed floating in the waves, moving to music only she can hear.

"Hey, Crystal, groovy dance," I say, grinning at her.

Waving her arms, she mermaid-dances in a circle around me. I laugh and hand her the joint.

I hear a hum of conversation and dance over to see what Nikki and Tony are up to. They're sitting on the stump chairs at the table. The bag of chips is open. They're taking chips out of the bag one at a time, holding them up to the candlelight, turning them this way and that, with looks of wonder on their faces as if they've never seen a chip before.

"So yellow . . . like really, really yellow . . ." Tony says.

"And pebbly," Nikki adds, running her fingers over the surface of the one in her hand.

"Should we eat one?" Tony says, and Nikki nods. They each stuff a chip into their mouths and chew slowly, eyes wide as they stare at each other. It seems to take them forever to finish chewing. Finally Tony says, "Crunchy!"

"Salty."

They reach into the bag for more chips and hold them up to the candlelight again.

I laugh out loud.

Nikki and Tony look at me in surprise. Then they grin and start laughing with me. I twirl around, flinging out my arms to take everyone in. "You guys are the greatest!"

"You too," Crystal says, still doing her seaweed dance. "Especially for getting us this cabin."

Zach looks up. "Yeah," he agrees with a grin.

"You can get it anytime, right?" Tony asks.

I drop my arms. "And if not, am I out of the club?" There's a bit of edge in my voice.

A second of silence, and then Zach laughs. "Of course not, don't be stupid."

I laugh too. "I knew that. I was just kidding."

"Hey, why don't we make it a club for real?" Gretchen asks. "The . . . the Party Club."

"Lame," Tony says. "The Pot and Booze Club."

"And mushrooms," Crystal puts in. "Don't forget the mushrooms."

"The ZNCMGT Club," Nikki says, mashing our initials together in one guttural sound.

"Gesundheit," Tony says, and we all shriek with laughter.

Zach opens the second mickey. Even Crystal indulges and weaves around tipsily. Tony changes the CD, putting on the Puff Adders, another screeching metal band with hammering drumbeats.

"You really like that scorching guitar, don't you?" I shout.

In response, Tony plays air guitar, jumping up and down like a crazed metalhead, nodding his head furiously, his black hair flying up and down. This makes me laugh so hard I nearly pee. I run outside and squat in the snow. I stay outside for a few minutes, looking at the shadow of that tall hemlock and remembering when it was Gwen's and my tepee.

When I come back inside, things are quieter. Everybody's reached that point where you feel too dazed and slow to do or say much of anything. Everybody sits or sways or stands for a minute, and then Nikki says, "I'm cold."

"Me too," Crystal says. "Let's start a fire."

"Yeah, let's," Gretchen says.

I'm cold too – the sweat I built up earlier is drying, and it really is chilly in the cabin – and I'm about to join the chorus, but a memory stops me. Gwen and I must have been nine or ten. We'd smuggled a bag of marshmallows out to the cabin – even though I was usually the ringleader, this was *her* idea; marshmallows were a forbidden treat since her mom was such a health-food freak. We'd started a fire in the woodstove, speared marshmallows on long sticks, and managed to roast a couple of them to perfectly charred blobs in the open firebox, when Bridget burst into the cabin.

"What do you girls think you're doing!" she shrieked.

Gwen blanched, trying to hide her sticky mouth, thinking she was in trouble over the marshmallows. Instead, Bridget poked the flaming chunks of wood apart and slammed the firebox door shut.

"You must never, ever start a fire in here without a grown-up!" she yelled. "It's not safe. This old woodstove was worn-out when we got it." She grabbed each of us by the arm. "Do you hear me?"

"Yes," we both said, lips trembling.

She hugged us to her, then sat with us until the fire was completely out.

Now, I say, "I don't know, guys. I don't think it's such a good idea."

"But I'm really cold," Nikki says. "Look at me, my teeth are chattering."

"Me too," Gretchen says, jumping up. "Is there any paper around?"

My head feels thick. "But the cabin's really old," I say. "And dry."

"Chill, Molly," Tony says.

Tony snaps a few slats off the broken chair. Meanwhile, Nikki's found an old magazine and is tearing out pages.

"I really don't think —" I try again, but before I know it, they're crumpling up the paper and laying the slats on top, and then there's a crackle, a smell of dust and creosote, and a little fire starts snapping away in the firebox.

"See? Isn't that nice?" Crystal asks, warming her hands.

"Mmm, that's better," Nikki says, drawing near.

Tony pulls off another slat and feeds it to the flames, which are burning vigorously now. Even I am drawn to the stove, grateful for the warmth on my face, feeling the iron surface turn from cold to warm to hot.

Tony yanks off the last slat. The fire's roaring now, eating the old, dry wood. He breaks off one of the chair legs. "We're going to have to find some more furniture," he jokes just as I hear a roar, like a plane taking off, inside the metal chimney that rises from the back of the woodstove. I notice that a portion of the pipe is glowing red. And then I notice that there's a small gap between that section and the adjoining one, where the metal's rusted away. Suddenly a spark flies out from the gap and lands on the floor.

"Guys! Look out!" I yell, stamping out the spark.

Tony, who's bent over putting the chair leg into the firebox, twists. "Oh no," he says as another, and then another spark flies out.

Crystal, the cedar fronds drooping in her hair, is frozen in place. Nikki, too, seems spellbound as she watches the stream of sparks.

"Guys, help!" I yell, jumping like a crazed insect from one spark here to another there, and there.

Everybody springs into action. Tony is trying to break apart the fire in the firebox. Nikki and Zach are helping me kill sparks. Crystal opens the cabin door. Gretchen starts screaming.

But the sparks are coming faster than we can catch them. One lands on my sleeve and I hear a sizzle as it burns a small hole in the fabric.

"Ow!" Nikki yelps as one falls on her bare arm.

One spark catches on the floor, and the old floorboard smolders for a moment before the smoke dies out. Then a larger one lands near the first and actually burns, flame darting up from the tinder-dry floor as if touched into life by a fairy wand – until Zach stamps it out.

We're running around, getting in each other's way, stumbling as we lurch from burning spot to burning spot, coughing as the smoke thickens, rubbing our eyes.

"Ow!" screams Crystal as she's burned on the cheek.

Tony is unable to quench the fire in the firebox.

"We've got to get out of here," sobs Gretchen, who's crying now. "Zach, come on!"

There's a crackling sound, and a chunk of the metal pipe that was glowing red-hot actually breaks off and falls to the floor. We all stand there, stunned, staring at this piece of metal, not quite able to believe that the chimney is falling apart. Then, hearing a louder roar, we turn and watch the gap as the flames roar up from the bottom part of the chimney pipe. It's like we have a sneak peek at a vertical orange inferno. As we watch, a burning clump of creosote shoots out of the gap and lands on the floor. Instantly it catches, and in a moment, flames are rolling along the length of the floorboard and licking up the wall. There's an explosion as the fire reaches the vodka bottle and the remaining booze bursts into flame, shooting from the bottle.

"Help!" Gretchen screams.

"We've got to get out of here before we're caught," Nikki says.

I whip off my hoodie and start batting at the flames. "Come on, guys, help me!" My eyes are stinging and I'm coughing.

Instead, they all edge toward the door.

"We can't just let it burn down!" I yell, flailing at the flames with my scorched hoodie. The fire is now creeping halfway up the wall, and it's three floorboards wide. I'm hopping to stay out of its path.

"I'm out of here," Tony says, bolting out the door, followed by Crystal and Nikki.

"Molly, don't be stupid," Zach says, grabbing a now-hysterical Gretchen.

"I can't – I've got to –" I hack, choking.

They're gone. I turn back. The fire now covers the width of the wall. One arm over my face, I run around, beating at the floor, the walls. I smell my hair singe. The soles of my sneakers smell like burning rubber. I know it's a losing battle, but I can't just give up. I can't do this to Andrew and Bridget.

Finally my hoodie is burned to a useless shred. My eyes are streaming, my arms ache, I'm gasping painful breaths. The fire has spread to a second wall and nearly the entire floor is burning.

I know I'm beaten. The only thing I can do is run — and hope the Torrances never find out I was here.

I dash across the burning floor, outside into the cool, damp air. I bend over, hands on knees, and cough and gasp, and black tears and snot and ash fly out of me and fall on a mound of snow.

I hear a loud crackle behind me. I don't turn. I don't have the strength to run. Instead, I stumble down the trail, wheezing, staggering, slipping on patches of snow. I hear a louder roar, an explosion of shattering glass, a crash and thud. I keep moving.

I've just reached the side road when I hear a siren, and then I see the twirling red lights of the Thor Falls volunteer fire truck. I force myself into an exhausted sprint, trying to reach the end of the road before they get here — and run straight into the head-lights of a cop car.

FIVE

Gwen opened her eyes. The ceiling was green. *That's weird,* she thought. *My ceiling's not green.*

Her eyes closed. Sleepily, the thought formed: *Then this must not be my room.*

Her eyes flew open.

Then where am I?

Her mind raced, trying to remember. And then – the snow, the noise, the wind. Her father.

The hospital. I must be in the hospital.

She turned – and there was her mother, sitting on a chair beside the bed, chin in hand, half-looking out the window at the dreary gray rain.

"Mom." It came out like a croak.

"Gwen! Oh, Gwennie . . ." Her mother seized her shoulders and held her close. "Honey, are you okay?"

"Dad?" was all Gwen could say.

Her mother laid her back down. "He's in Vancouver."

"Alive?"

Her mother looked at her in amazement. "You don't know?"

Gwen shook her head.

"Oh, Gwennie." Her voice shook. "Yes, he's alive . . ."

Thank God, thank God, oh thank you, God.

"But he's hurt. Badly. They don't know how badly yet. He has some broken ribs. One lung collapsed. They're doing tests."

Oh God.

"Where am I?"

Again her mother looked surprised. "Norse River General."

"How'd I get here? How'd Dad get out?"

"You don't remember?"

Gwen shook her head. "All I remember is the snow . . . the noise . . . then he was gone."

"Oh, Gwen, to think you went through that." Her mother cried quietly against the bed for a minute. "It was Simon. Simon, bless his heart. He was out on his snowmobile –"

Gwen nodded. Now she remembered that they had talked to Simon, right before . . .

"He saw *you* go down, then Dad. He yanked you out, then started digging where he thought Dad was. Took a while, but he finally found him. Thank God for those beepers!" She collected herself and went on. "Dad seemed to be in worse shape, so Simon took him down first. Called emergency services on his cell phone. They sent a helicopter. Then he went back for you. They brought both of you here, but the doctors decided

Dad needed intensive care, so they flew him on to Vancouver."

Intensive care. Gwen imagined her father lying inside a big plastic bubble, needles sticking in his arms, wires trailing to blinking machines.

"If it hadn't been for Simon . . ." Her mom put her head down and wept into her hands.

Gwen cried too, turning her face into the pillow. If it hadn't been for Simon, her father would be dead. And it would all be her fault.

Her mom blew her nose. "Don't you remember coming down, Gwennie?"

Gwen shook her head. Vaguely she remembered loud noises coming closer and closer – she had thought it was another avalanche – and cold and pain and voices and hands lifting her and then blackness.

"Am I hurt?"

Her mom brightened. "That's the amazing thing. They took X-rays right away – you were still out of it . . ."

Now that she was reminded of it, Gwen vaguely recalled being pushed and pulled and wheeled around.

"And even though you're bruised all over, nothing's broken. And as far as they can tell, there're no internal injuries. They say it's a miracle."

I got away free and he got hurt.

"Were you there, Mom? Did you see him?"

Her mother nodded.

"Did you talk to him?" *What did he tell you?*

Her mother shook her head. "He was asleep." She gave a strangled laugh. "But if he had been awake, I would have killed him."

"Why?"

"For putting himself in danger – and *you*." Her voice cracked. "For risking your life!"

Gwen turned her head to the side. If her mother only knew. It wasn't her father who had risked their lives.

Her mother gave the same anguished laugh. "Let's let him get well, and then I'll kill him."

"What about me?" Gwen asked. "How long will I be here?"

Her mother shrugged. "I don't know, honey. The doctor may want to examine you again, now that you're fully awake, just to make sure everything's okay. Then I guess you can come home."

As if on cue, the curtain around Gwen's bed was pushed aside and a man in a white hospital coat, a stethoscope around his neck, walked in. He looked familiar.

"Oh, Dr. Chan," her mother said. "I was just telling Gwen that you X-rayed her and everything looked okay."

Dr. Chan, that was it. Gwen remembered him. He'd taken Percy's tonsils out a couple of years earlier. He'd been really nice. He'd given Gwen Popsicles too, understanding how she felt with everyone fussing over her little brother.

Now Dr. Chan said, "How are you feeling, Gwen?"

"Okay, I guess."

"That's good. I can tell you, you are a very lucky young lady. To go through what you did and escape with just bruises is incredible."

Lucky. Right. "I know."

"So can Gwen come home, Dr. Chan?" her mom asked.

"Yes. I don't see any need to keep her here. I'm sure you'll want to rest and get your strength back, Gwen. After all, you're pretty banged up. But you'll be more comfortable doing that at home."

Gwen nodded, wondering what home would be like without her dad there. Wondering when he *would* be there. Or *if.* No. She cut off the thought.

Dr. Chan signed some forms, then leaned down and shook Gwen's hand. "Take care, Gwen. And no more skiing for a while." He chuckled.

Gwen's mother went to fetch Gwen's clothes from a closet. Gwen swung her legs over the edge of the bed and stood up. "Ow!" she said, and sat back down.

Dr. Chan, who was nearly out the door, and her mother both turned.

"What's the matter, honey?" her mother said, hurrying over.

Dr. Chan came back. "What's wrong, Gwen?"

"My leg. It hurt. When I stood up."

"Where?" Dr. Chan asked.

Gwen pointed to her right leg and traced from her outer ankle to her knee. "From there to there."

"That's strange," Dr. Chan said. "You do have a large bruise on that thigh, but that shouldn't cause pain just from putting weight on the leg." He had Gwen lie down, then began to press gently, starting at the top of the thigh and moving down. "Tell me if it hurts. There? There?"

Gwen shook her head, though she winced when he got near the bruise.

Dr. Chan continued to press. Gwen kept saying, "No . . . no . . ." All the way down to her ankle. Nothing.

He shrugged. "Let's get you up again and see how it feels."

Supporting Gwen under the elbow, he helped her to her feet. As soon as she stood on her right foot, the same pain shot up her leg, from her ankle to above her knee. "Ow!"

Dr. Chan shook his head. "I can't understand it. The X-rays were clear. You're sure it's not just stiffness? After all, you've been lying in bed."

"Yes!" Gwen shot back. She was a dancer. She knew the difference between stiffness and pain.

Dr. Chan had her walk, bend her knees, rock back and forth, side to side. The pain returned when she shifted her weight from left to right, when she pliéd her right knee, when she flexed her right ankle, when she rose on her right foot.

"And it's just on the one side?" he asked.

Tears stinging her eyes, Gwen nodded. Just the right. The leg she could kick higher, point harder, leap onto better. Her strong leg.

Dr. Chan helped her lie down. "I'm baffled, Gwen. I can't understand how we could have missed something big enough to cause that much pain, but, just to be sure, I'll order an MRI. Maybe it'll turn up something the X-rays missed." He filled out a form, then left.

After her mother had gone – back to Vancouver, to consult with her father's doctors and sit at his bedside – Gwen pushed off the covers. *Had* she imagined it? She stood up. *Ow!* Shooting pain, from ankle to knee.

She sank back onto the bed. The throbbing faded. She fell into a restless sleep . . .

Her first dance class. She was six, a bundle of restless motion, constantly skipping, climbing, running. Her mother had signed her up for modern dance, no doubt hoping she'd work off some of that energy.

She walked into the dance studio, mirrors along one wall and a barre along another, beams of sunlight shining down through a skylight and illuminating the worn wooden boards of the floor. A beautiful room, with a warm, dry smell – and so much space to move!

Then she looked around and realized she was different. Her mother, not knowing proper dance attire, had sent her to class in a dress. A dress! All the other kids were in proper leotards and tights, seashell pink, turquoise, black. Quickly she tore off her shoes and socks, seeing the others in bare feet or ballet slippers. She stayed at the side of the room, clinging to the barre, certain that the teacher would send her away in disgrace.

But Mrs. Truman came in, with her frizzy hair in a bun and a flowing black skirt, and smiled at everyone; perhaps she had a brighter smile for the distressed little girl in the dress. She put on music, something tinkly and merry, and said, "Dance to the music. However it makes you feel, whatever it tells you to do, just dance."

Most of the other kids looked around self-consciously, looking for *the right way,* waiting for someone to begin, wanting to imitate and not do it wrong. But Gwen listened. She heard water. She heard leaves. She saw elves frolicking in a glen, cleverly hiding from nosy, poking humans. Her dress disappeared, and she was clad in green, the dark green of leaves at full summer. She lifted her arms. She took tiny running steps, a twirl, a leap, peering over her shoulder, zigzagging this way and that, behind a tree, behind a rock – quick, before they see us!

When the music stopped, Gwen, surprised, came back to class, to herself. She felt Mrs. Truman's eyes on her.

Gwen thought about the dance she'd just done. She could not have recreated the steps. She just knew that she had been there, in the glen, behind the tree, inside the music.

———

Gwen awakened. Her muscles were straining: she must have been dancing in her sleep.

Dancing.

She thought of her leg. How could she dance on that leg? She couldn't, not with that shooting pain, that weakness. She'd have no strength, no balance, no lift.

No dancing.

A spasm gripped her middle and tears sprang to her eyes.

How can I live without dancing?

She couldn't. It would be a nonlife. A dead life.

She sobbed, pushing her face into her pillow to muffle the cries.

Then a thought struck: No matter how bad this was, it wasn't as bad as the shape her father was in. Not even close.

That made her stop crying. How could she feel sorry for herself when he was suffering? And it was her doing.

She wondered if he was conscious. If he was in pain. If he was still alive. *Oh God, please,* she thought, *don't let him die, let him get well, I'll do anything.*

Anything.

She slept, was wheeled down for the MRI, pushed away the food they brought her, slept some more. When she next awoke, her mother was sitting in the chair again. She looked exhausted, as if she hadn't slept in days. The circles under her eyes were darker, her cheeks more hollow.

"Gwennie," she said when Gwen stirred. She kissed Gwen on the forehead and helped her sit up. "How are you feeling?"

"The same." Gwen saw disappointment flit across her mother's face. "How's Dad?"

"He might need surgery. They're doing tests."

Surgery was good, Gwen told herself. It meant that something could be fixed. Didn't it?

The curtain was pushed aside and Dr. Chan peeked in. "Gwen? Oh, Mrs. Torrance, I'm glad you're here. I have the results of Gwen's MRI." He opened a file and looked at it briefly. "It confirmed what the X-rays showed. There's no sign of damage."

"But it hurts."

"Same place?"

Nod.

"Any worse?"

"A little."

"I don't know what to tell you, Gwen. Your kneecap looks healthy. The tibia and fibula are sound. There's no sign of cartilage or ligament damage."

"So why does it hurt so much?"

"I don't know." He glanced at her mother, then sat down on the edge of the bed. "There's only one other explanation I can think of. Maybe it's stress. After all, you've been through a traumatic experience —"

"I'm not making it up!"

"I didn't say that. But stress can do funny things to the mind –"

"There's something wrong with my leg," Gwen insisted.

Dr. Chan shook his head. "Gwen, I assure you that there is nothing medically wrong with your leg."

"So I'm crazy?"

"Of course not. That's not what I said. It's just that stress can cause all kinds of symptoms – and in the absence of an obvious injury, perhaps that's an explanation."

Gwen slouched down and folded her arms across her chest.

"I suggest we monitor it," Dr. Chan said. "See how things progress. Maybe an injury will show up, and then we'll know how to treat it. Or maybe the pain will clear up by itself."

Gwen didn't answer. Into the silence, her mother said, "Then Gwen can come home, Dr. Chan?"

He nodded, rising. "There doesn't seem to be anything we can do here. And Gwen, whatever it is, I'm sure it's not serious. There's no reason to stay off your feet. You can exercise normally. In fact, exercise would probably help. I mean, I wouldn't go overboard – you've still got some nasty bruises – but you can be as active as you like."

"But not dance," Gwen said under her breath.

"Gwen!" her mother said.

"Gwen," Dr. Chan said. He waited until she looked at him. "There is no reason you can't dance."

Gwen rolled to face the wall. It didn't matter what he said. She knew she couldn't dance.

She heard her mother's footsteps follow Dr. Chan's across the room. "What's the matter with her, doctor?" her mother whispered. "It's not like Gwen to make things up."

"She's not exactly making it up, Mrs. Torrance. I believe she's suffering from post-traumatic stress as a result of the avalanche – which is understandable. It was a pretty traumatic event. And I suppose that somehow the stress is manifesting itself in this symptom. As the memory of the avalanche fades, the pain probably will too."

"I hope so."

"I'm sure it will. These types of reactions are not uncommon. They usually resolve themselves. But if she doesn't get over it in a few weeks, bring her in and we'll do a psychiatric evaluation. We don't want to let this go on too long."

Gwen pressed her lips together. There was no way she was going to let some shrink probe around inside her head.

Gwen's mother came back to her beside. Taking a look at Gwen, she said, "You heard?"

Gwen nodded. "You think I'm making it up too?"

Her mother hesitated. "I don't know."

"Mom!"

"Well, I know you wouldn't lie, but – I don't know what to think. Maybe it's the trauma, like he said."

"It's real."

"Okay, I believe you. But Gwennie, what's this about not dancing?"

"I can't dance. My leg is too sore."

"Sure, maybe for a little while, until it gets better –"

Gwen shook her head.

"Gwen, you can't give up on your dancing!"

"I can't dance."

"But you love it so –"

"Forget it, Mom. I know my body. Just leave me alone about it, okay?"

There was a pause. "Okay. Can you be ready in fifteen minutes?"

Gwen nodded.

"All right. I'll be waiting at the nurses' station."

Gwen threw her few items of clothing into a bag, then limped into the bathroom. She looked at herself in the mirror. She looked like hell – her face was pale, there were deep shadows under her eyes, and her hair hung limply. Automatically she gathered it up and twisted it into a knot, the same knot she'd made for dance class for so many years. Then, realizing what she was doing, she loosened the knot and let her hair hang down again. Tears filled her eyes. She gripped the sink, staring at her reflection.

Something caught her eye. A roll of adhesive tape and a pair of scissors were on the windowsill. A nurse must have left them there.

Gwen picked up the scissors. She lifted a hank of hair. Tears rolling down her cheeks, she cut. A clump of hair fell into the sink. She lifted the next piece of hair.

SIX

I'm sitting in the Thor Falls police station. It's not much of a station. It's more of a storefront, really, with a booking area out front, a couple of offices, a detention room with a table and chairs, and a cell – only it isn't even a real jail cell with bars and stuff, just a locked room with a cot and toilet.

I can't stop shaking. It's not cold, or fear, though I'm plenty scared. And it's not burns. I mean, my eyebrows and hair are singed and frizzed, and there're angry red marks around my nose ring and eyebrow stud and earrings where the metal heated up and burned me. But aside from blisters on my hands, and a weird case of sunburn on my face, and speckled spots on my arms and back where sparks scorched through my clothes, I'm not even burned, which is amazing.

No, it's shock. And anger. Because of Gwen. She must have been the one who called the cops. Who else could it have been? Her house is closest. She must have seen us going into the cabin. It's bad enough that we're not friends anymore, but for her to rat me out? I can't believe she'd be so rotten.

I'm in the detention room. The cop who arrested me, Constable Sawchuk, is across the table from me, and my parents are on either side. It wasn't pretty when they got to the station. My mom ran in, eyes red, and wailed, "Oh, Molly, how could you!" And my dad, grim-faced as ever, grabbed my arm and said through gritted teeth, "Just wait till we get home."

I don't know Constable Sawchuk; he must be new to Thor Falls. Youngish. Blond hair cut to razor sharpness. Crisp collar and shiny shoes. Looks like he was born following the rules.

He places both palms on the table. "Now, Molly, I'm going to ask you some questions and I want you to tell me the truth."

I nod.

"What were you doing in the Torrances' cabin?"

I hesitate. "Drinking."

There's a sharp intake of breath from my father, but he doesn't say anything.

"What else?"

How much worse can it get? "Smoking pot."

A gasp from my mom.

"Who was with you?"

This is the question I've been dreading. The question I haven't even wanted to ask myself. I feel sick every time my mind veers near it. Why did they run? Why didn't they help me? Why did they leave me to get caught?

They were scared, I tell myself. They were freaked out. The bloody cabin was burning down! They didn't just abandon me. I won't believe that they did. And I won't rat them out.

"No one," I say quietly.

"Molly!" my mom says.

"Molly, tell the truth," my dad snaps.

"Mr. and Mrs. Norquist, I'm going to have to ask you to let Molly answer the questions," Constable Sawchuk says.

He turns back to me. "I'll ask you again, Molly. Who was with you at the cabin?"

"No one." Louder this time.

He folds his hands. "The cabin collapsed, so it's going to take several days to sift through the remains to see what's there. But one of the firefighters told me he saw the melted lump of what used to be a ghetto blaster in the ashes. Are you telling me that you hauled that down there to listen to music and drink booze and smoke marijuana all by yourself?"

I can't look him in the eye. "Yes."

An impatient sigh from my father.

"And how do you account for the fact that there were several different sets of footprints in the snow?"

I shrug. "Maybe some other people used the cabin before –" *us,* I almost say "– before me."

He leans back in his chair. "Molly, you do realize that this is a very serious situation, don't you? Aside from the underage drinking and marijuana misdemeanors, you're looking at significant charges related to the destruction of the cabin. The punishment could be severe."

I don't trust myself to speak. I nod.

"So protecting your friends or whoever else was there isn't doing yourself or them any favors. They need to come forward and take responsibility for their actions."

They will, I think. *When they hear I'm in trouble, they will.*

"It was just me."

He makes an impatient sound. "We'll leave that for now. How did the fire start?"

"I – I was cold, so I started a fire in the old woodstove."

"What happened?"

"The chimney started roaring, and sparks started shooting out –" I have to stop and swallow. "And then a chunk of pipe fell off, and a ball of fire shot out, and the floor caught. I tried to stop it –" I hear my voice trembling. "But I couldn't. I just couldn't."

He nods. "Why did you run?"

"I couldn't save the cabin." I pause. "I – I was afraid of getting caught."

He looks at me for a long moment. Then he says, "Molly Ann Norquist, you are charged with trespassing and destruction of property."

I gasp. *Charged.* Until now, it hasn't seemed real. *Will I go to jail? Will I have a record? What will happen to me?*

He tells us to report to youth court in Norse River the next day. Then he releases me into the custody of my parents.

We step outside. The sky is that purple-blue shade just before dawn. There's a faint whiff of smoke on the air.

"You're a disgrace."

"How could you?"

"You're ruining your life."

We're in the kitchen. My mom's sobbing, her head on her arms, and my dad's pacing, slapping the back of one hand into the palm of the other as he bites off each word.

He stops. Points to me. "Are you going to stick to this charade of being alone?"

"Yes."

"Oh, Molly." My mom lifts her head with a moan. "You know that's not true."

I don't answer. My friends wouldn't squeal on me. I won't squeal on them.

"And how could you do this to Bridget and Andrew?" my mom asks.

That brings tears to my eyes.

"I'm telling you now, Molly," my dad says. "The party's over. You've been running wild, but it's going to stop. No more drinking. No more drugs. No more being out late."

"But it's spring break –"

"I don't care if it's a bloody national holiday. From now on, you will stay in every night, and if you go out, we will know where you are and who you're with and what you're doing. Is that clear?"

Before, I've been able to sneak out, get around my punishments. Something tells me I'm not going to be able to this time. My life is going to be hell. "Yes."

A clock radio goes off upstairs. My sisters' alarm. Trust them to keep their alarm set when there's no school.

A few minutes later they come downstairs, two identical twelve year olds in their nightgowns. They take after my mom, petite and slender, everything small: ears, noses, hands, feet. I'm like my dad: tall and solid, with a strong nose and big hands and feet. We both have that fair skin that freckles in the summer and blooms with two red spots in the cheeks when we're excited. Or mad. Which my dad is right now.

Joanna and Juliet take one look at the three of us and ask, "What happened?"

My dad tells them, leaving out the bits about the intoxicants.

Joanna, who's the older one by a few minutes, looks at me in disgust. In perfect imitation of our mother, she says, "Oh, Molly, how could you?"

I don't answer.

Joanna rolls her eyes. "I can't believe you're my sister. This is so embarrassing."

"Yeah, it's really all about you, Joanna," I snap. If I weren't in so much trouble, I'd be glad I was freaking her out.

"Well, everybody talks and it rubs off on us."

"Tough!"

"Girls!" my mother says.

Joanna shoots me a dirty look. Silence falls. Then Juliet comes over and touches my shoulder. "Are you okay, Moll?"

These are the first kind words anyone's said to me. Tears sting my eyes. I run upstairs and throw myself on my bed.

The next week is hell. The day after my arrest, I appear before a judge in youth court in Norse River. The lawyer for the government reads out the charges against me — they sound even worse in the courtroom than they did in the police station — and the judge sets bail at one thousand dollars, which my parents have to put up to make sure I'll appear for my sentencing.

Then we see a defense lawyer, who advises me to plead guilty. For one thing, he says, the evidence against me is pretty overwhelming. For another, if I plead not guilty, the case will have to go to trial, and that's the last thing I want.

This whole time, my parents say nothing to me except "Get in the car" and "Get out of the car." I'm glad. I couldn't talk, anyway. I don't want to make excuses. I don't want to chat. I don't want to see anyone. All I can think about is how sorry I feel about Bridget and Andrew's cabin, and how furious I am at Gwen.

It's a week later. I'm back in the Norse River municipal hall with my parents, waiting in a hallway. Today's my sentencing. I'm wearing a skirt and blouse and nylons, and it feels freaking strange. I can't remember the last time I was dressed like this.

The singed bits have been cut out of my hair, so it's a little lop-sided. Still, I'm as presentable as I can be, and I hope it helps.

I'm so nervous I can barely swallow.

Someone calls my name, and my parents and I go into the courtroom. There's a different judge this time. She's about my parents' age, with a thin face, short brown hair, and a no-nonsense expression to go with her black robe. A name card on her desk reads "Judge Nancy Peters."

Constable Sawchuk is there, and so are the government lawyer and my lawyer. We stand in front of the judge. I smooth out my skirt.

"Molly Ann Norquist, how do you plead?" she asks.

"Guilty, Your Honor," says my lawyer.

I sit. Constable Sawchuk runs through what happened, with Judge Peters asking questions every once in a while. When he finishes, the judge asks, "Are the Torrances pressing charges?"

"Well, Your Honor, Mr. Torrance is unavailable at the moment. He's in the hospital in Vancouver."

Andrew? In the hospital?

"Oh?" the judge says.

"Yes, he was seriously injured in an avalanche."

Oh my God.

"Oh, yes, I heard about that," Judge Peters says. "On Mount Odin, wasn't it?"

Constable Sawchuk nods.

"What about Mrs. Torrance?"

"I did speak to her, and she said she would not press charges against Molly."

"Did she consent to compensation in the form of community work service?"

"Yes, Your Honor."

Judge Peters turns to me. "Stand please, Molly."

I do.

"You understand that this is a serious matter?"

I can hardly find my voice. "Yes . . . Your Honor."

She consults some papers. "I understand that you are claiming that you acted alone – that you and you alone were using the Torrances' cabin and that you and you alone started the fire that got out of control. Is that correct?"

"Yes, Your Honor."

I feel my parents stiffen behind me. I ignore it.

The judge folds her hands and gazes at me. "It was a very foolish and wrongheaded thing you did, to use someone's property without permission, and in such a reckless and careless manner. You are lucky to have escaped with your life, not to mention the fact that you endangered the lives of those who lived nearby."

She pauses. I'm not sure if I'm supposed to say anything. And what can I say, anyway? I know I'm lucky. I'm so sorry that my sorriness is as big as the world. How do I put that into words?

Thankfully I don't have to. She goes on, "However, in light of your age, and the fact that you have no previous record, and the fact that the Torrances are not pressing charges and have agreed to compensation, I am placing you on probation and sentencing you to thirty hours of community service, to be served at the discretion of the Torrance family."

"What does that mean?" I ask.

"It means that you will report to the Torrance home and do thirty hours of work for them. You're too young to get a job, so you can't repay them financially. But this will, in small measure, provide compensation to them."

"What kind of work?"

"That's entirely up to the Torrances. I understand that the cabin has been demolished, with no chance of salvage. And in any case, it would be too dangerous to have you working in the ruins. But I'm sure there are other chores you can do. Gardening. Housework. I'll assign you a youth court officer, who will work out with them what they'd like you to do."

I can't face them, I think. But of course I don't say it.

Judge Peters leans forward. "I hope you'll learn from this, Molly. Reflect on your behavior, your safety, your sense of responsibility. And, even though they don't exist," she adds drily, "the people you choose to call your friends."

"Yes, Your Honor."

With my parents I go upstairs and find the office number Judge Peters gave us. I knock.

"Come in," a voice calls. It sounds familiar.

I open the door.

Damn. My youth court officer is Cal Robichaud.

He's the father of my friend Susie. My former friend Susie, that is. We used to be friends, but we drifted apart. Now she's Gwen's best friend. But I've been to Susie's house dozens of times, jumping on her trampoline, going to her birthday parties. Her dad is a big, hefty guy with a round, kind face and the same reddish-blond hair as Susie, only he's going bald. I remember that he has one of those rumble-from-the-belly kind of laughs. I always liked him.

I knew Cal had something to do with the law, and that he went up and down the coast and sometimes worked out of an office at the police station in Thor Falls. But I never knew he was a youth court officer. Now I'm going to have to report to him? God, how embarrassing.

He looks surprised when we come through the door. "Larry . . . Lynn . . . Molly . . . what are you doing here?"

"Trouble, Cal, I'm sorry to say," my father says.

Cal gives him a puzzled look. I hand him the papers Judge Peters gave me and he reads them over. His cheeks turn pink. "I see," he says, avoiding my eye. "I'd heard about that fire, but I had no idea. . . . Well, Molly, it looks like we're going to be spending some time together." He seems even more embarrassed than me.

We sit down, and he explains how my probation will work. For starters, I'll have a curfew. It's to be set by my parents – I can just see myself in by seven every night. I'm not to consume any alcohol or nonprescription drugs. As for the thirty hours of community work service, he'll accompany me to the Torrances' house and discuss with them – or, since Andrew's in the hospital, with Bridget – what kind of work she'd like me to do. From time to time, Cal will check in with my parents to make sure I'm obeying my curfew, and with Bridget to make sure I'm doing my service. When the thirty hours are done, my probation will be finished. And I'll have a record.

He makes arrangements to meet me at Bridget's the following afternoon.

And so begins my sentence.

SEVEN

Gwen came home. The first thing she did was take all of her dance clothes – her leotards and tights and yoga pants and jazz shoes – stuff them in a bag, and throw the bag onto the floor of her closet.

Then she went from room to room and gathered up all the pictures of herself dancing.

There was one taken at her first recital, when she was six. The children were dressed like mice, with pipe cleaner whiskers and felt ears. In the picture, they stood in a row, their mittened hands held up in front like paws. Gwen was in the middle, Carley beside her. Taking the framed picture down from the mantel, Gwen remembered that performance. The dancers were supposed to go down the line, repeating a movement one at a time: first a jump, then a turn, then a wiggle. But when it was Carley's turn, she just stood there, dazzled by the bright lights and people watching. And Gwen had to wait for Carley to jump before *she* could jump – because that was what Mrs. Truman had said. So Gwen waited. But Carley didn't move. Gwen began to fret. Everyone was waiting. The sequence was stuck. Carley still stood there, smiling vaguely at the audience. Finally Gwen leaned over and whispered loudly, "Jump!" Startled, Carley jumped, then turned, then wiggled, and Gwen was able to perform her jump. It was only years later that she understood why the audience had burst out laughing.

On through the house. Pictures of her leaping, arms upflung; leaning forward in a graceful arabesque; stretching to the ceiling, the sky, the stars. Photos of her as a swan, as a clown, as a flamenco dancer in a black lace mantilla, as the fog, draped in a blue-gray cape. Her favorite picture captured her performing the dance she herself had choreographed to the passionate Brazilian music of Heitor Villa-Lobos, caught as she was about to turn, body twisted, arms curved back across her chest, head turned to look over her shoulder as if facing into the forever-parabola of that turn. She gathered them all, from the living room mantel, the hallway, the fridge, her parents' dresser, her own bedroom wall, and she stashed them, facedown, next to the bag on the floor of her closet.

Her mother fixed her a bed in the spare room on the main floor so she wouldn't have to climb the stairs. Even with the cane she had brought home from the hospital, though, her leg still ached. Only when she was sitting or lying down did the pain go away. So she sat. She sat in the easy chair in the living room, looking out the bay window at the sea below, watching the waves roll in, roll out, watching clouds gather and blow away, watching fishing boats appear on one side of the window frame and disappear behind the other. She sat very still, her only movement her fingers touching the shaggy, uneven ends of her hair, and tried not to think about what was hidden in her closet.

It didn't work.

Sitting there, she remembered the first time she knew she wanted to be a choreographer. She was seven years old and had been taking classes with Mrs. Truman for about a year. One day after class she'd realized that she'd left her mittens in the dance studio and had gone back to get them. Mrs. Truman was still there, alone, with some music on, dancing. Gwen had stayed in the doorway, not realizing she was hidden.

The music was lively and loud, and Mrs. Truman, watching herself in the mirror, took big, swooping steps, swinging her arms. Then the music got soft and light; it made you want to go on tippy-toes. Mrs. Truman did little, quick turns, first one way, then the other, always watching herself in the mirror with a small frown on her face.

Gwen stared. Was Mrs. Truman practicing a new dance? Would she show it to her students sometime? And why didn't she look happy? Gwen didn't know the answer, but she could tell that Mrs. Truman was concentrating, and she knew she shouldn't interrupt. She stayed where she was, quiet.

Mrs. Truman started the music again. This time, instead of

the swooping steps, she traced a circle of joyous leaps all around the room. At the open doorway, she stopped short. "Gwen! What are you doing here?"

By now Gwen had forgotten all about her mittens. "What are you doing, Mrs. Truman?"

"Choreographing."

"Chor – ee – what?"

"Making a dance."

"Making a dance," Gwen repeated. Didn't dances just exist, ready-made, waiting for someone to pluck them out of the air and dance them? She felt a pang of disappointment. It took away some of the magic to learn that dances were *made*.

But then a new thought came to her. If Mrs. Truman could make up dances, other people could too. *She* could. She had all these things inside her – leaps and skips and twirls, silly wiggles and graceful swoops – and she'd never known what to do with them. Until now. She could pull these things out of herself and put them together in a real, proper dance. She turned to go.

"Gwen?" Mrs. Truman was holding up her mittens. "Forget something?"

Gwen giggled. "Oops."

That evening, speaking carefully so she would correctly say the new word Mrs. Truman had taught her, she announced to her parents, "I am going to be a chor-e-o-gra-pher."

She hadn't stopped making up dances since. In the living room, on the street, at the playground. One time, she and her dad had been grocery shopping, and she was making up a dance about a tornado. As she twirled down the cereal aisle, she'd knocked down an entire display of corn flakes, boxes and boxes crashing down from a carefully arranged pyramid. The store manager had hollered. Her dad had apologized and, playing the stern parent, scolded her. But once out in the parking lot, they had looked at each other and burst out laughing.

A couple of years later, she'd read Carl Sandburg's poem "Fog," and the words "The fog comes on little cat feet" had made her feel like creeping, pouncing, tiptoeing. She'd made up a dance, all stealthy movements floating on air. Mrs. Truman liked the dance so much that she asked Gwen to teach it to the class, and they performed it at their final concert. Gwen still remembered when Mrs. Truman announced, "And now we'd like to present 'Fog,' created by our very own young choreographer, Gwen Torrance."

Choreographer.

And Dancemakers was going to take her to a new level.

But Dancemakers was gone. She was no longer a dancer. Now she was a gimp with a cane.

A few days after coming home, Gwen sat in the living room, looking at the rain outside. That was all it had been doing the last few days; the snow was nearly gone, almost as if it had never existed.

If only, she thought, watching the downpour.

There was a tap at the kitchen window. Percy was upstairs, and her mom was asleep, having arrived home from Vancouver late the night before. She'd asked Gwen if she wanted to come, but Gwen had begged off, using her leg as an excuse. There was no way she could have faced her dad.

Gwen pushed herself up and limped to the door.

"Sally!" she said as her neighbor came in, swathed in a rain poncho with a strange hump on her back, the two boys crowding around her legs. She held a large pot in both hands.

"Gwennie," Sally panted. She put the pot on the stove, kicked off her rubber boots, and whipped off the poncho to reveal a sleeping Tanya in a baby sling on her back. Turning to Gwen, Sally opened her arms. Tears briefly stung Gwen's eyes as she felt the warmth of Sally's chest, the tug of her embrace.

Paul yanked on the hem of Gwen's sweatshirt. "Percy here?"

Gwen nodded. "Upstairs."

Paul grabbed his little brother's arm. "Come on, Jasp!"

"Percy might not be in the mood –" Sally began, but they were heading to the stairs before she could finish. She grinned at Gwen. Then her smile faded. "Holy, Gwennie, you look awful."

Gwen looked down at the shapeless sweatshirt and baggy sweatpants she'd taken to wearing around the house.

"I don't mean your clothes," Sally said, giving Gwen an exasperated look. "I mean *you*. Have you been eating?"

Before Gwen could answer, her mother came into the kitchen, yawning and rubbing her eyes. "Sally! What's up?"

Sally indicated the pot. "Brought you some clam chowder."

"Oh, Sal, that's so kind."

"Kind my behind," Sally said, laughing. When she laughed, her round belly shook and her eyes disappeared as her cheeks bunched up. "Simon took the boys down to the beach so I could have some peace, and they brought back such a haul of clams, I didn't know what to do with them."

Gwen's mom took the lid off the pot and sniffed. "Mmm . . . I love your clam chowder."

Gwen did too. Sally's chowder, made according to her grand-mother's Coast Salish recipe, was more stew than soup, loaded with clams, kelp, potatoes, and wild onions. *Too bad,* Gwen thought, *I have no appetite these days.* A couple of pieces of toast, a few cups of tea, the odd pear or banana – that was about all she could manage.

Tanya stirred in the sling, her tiny booties kicking to either side. She squeaked, growled, then straightened, her fine black hair stick-ing out every which way. She was screwing up her face to cry when she popped her head over Sally's shoulder and saw Bridget and Gwen. Then she burst into a smile. "Ga!" she said, raising her arms.

"I'll take her," Gwen said, unzipping the sling and lifting Tanya out.

"Whew," Sally said, rolling her shoulders. "That kid takes after her mama." She laughed again.

"Here, let me make tea," Gwen's mom said, but Sally pushed her into a chair.

"Sit," she said. "You look beat."

"I am beat," Bridget said.

Sally filled the kettle. "So, how's Andrew?"

Gwen froze. She started to edge out of the room with the baby. Surely Tanya needed to play on the living room floor, right away.

Before her mother could answer, though, there was another knock on the kitchen door. Sally, who was closest, answered it. "Robert," she said, grinning. "Come on in."

Her brother-in-law, Simon's brother and fishing partner, stared at her, shaking the rain off his canvas jacket. "What are you doing here?"

"Same thing you are," Sally said, pointing at the parcel in his hands.

"Oh yeah," he said, blushing a little. He was the shier of the two brothers, the more serious. Gwen knew where her friend Danny, Robert's son, got his quietness from. Gwen had fished off the dock or scavenged on the beach with Danny many times when they were younger, and he could go all day without saying more than a few words. *Comforting,* she thought now.

Robert lay his brown paper–wrapped parcel on the table and opened it to reveal a whole salmon, sliced into inch-thick steaks, seasoned with lemon and herbs.

"Thought you could use this, what with all the to-ing and fro-ing," he said, taking off his ball cap and rotating it in his hands. "All you have to do is pop it in the oven for ten minutes."

"Oh, Robert," Gwen's mom said, rising and giving him a hug. He hugged her back awkwardly, then turned and patted Gwen on the cheek and kissed his niece.

"Sit, Robert," Sally said, so he did, first placing his jacket on a hook and his rubber boots on the mat next to Sally's. The kitchen took on the familiar smell of damp wool.

The kettle whistled. Sally bustled about, clattering cups, getting the milk and sugar.

"So . . . how's Andrew?" Robert asked.

Gwen darted a glance at her mother. The expression on her face made Gwen look away.

Bridget pushed a hand through her hair. "His liver's swollen. He's in a lot of pain."

For a second, Gwen felt dizzy. She clung to the baby, taking deep breaths.

"What are the doctors saying –" Sally began.

There was another tap at the door. It opened, and Cynthia Robichaud, the mother of Gwen's friend Susie, poked her head around. Plump and dimpled, she had the same wavy, strawberry-blond hair as Susie, frizzy now in the humidity.

"Bridget!" she said. "I wasn't sure if you were back." Then, coming inside, "Sally, Robert, Gwen. Hi."

"Join the party," Sally said with a laugh, pulling up another chair.

Adding her wet jacket to the row of others, Cynthia deposited four loaves of bread on the table. A fresh-baked, yeasty smell filled the kitchen. "Made you a few loaves," she said. "Whole wheat, raisin, rye, and rosemary-walnut. Figured you didn't have time to shop, let alone bake."

Gwen's mother burst into tears. "Oh, Cynthia . . ."

"Don't be silly," Susie's mom said, patting Bridget on the shoulder. "What are neighbors for? Actually, I came to see if you need anything from the store. I'm going, anyway, so give me your grocery list."

Laughing at herself, Gwen's mom broke into a fresh bout of weeping.

"Here, drink your tea," Sally said, pushing a cup into Bridget's hands and handing mugs to the others.

Gwen stood near the doorway to the living room, holding Tanya, who was amusing herself by grabbing handfuls of Gwen's hair and pulling. Gwen longed to get out of the kitchen. There were too many people, too much talk. It would be rude, she knew; they were old friends. But she couldn't stand it. Maybe now, when no one was looking –

No. Cynthia came over to her. Trapped. Placing her hand on Gwen's shoulder, Cynthia asked, "How are you, sweetheart?"

Gwen stiffened. "All right."

Cynthia shook her head. "What you went through! It must have been horrible. It's a miracle you both got out alive, isn't it?"

Gwen nodded. *I've got to get out of here,* she thought. But she couldn't, not while they were all looking at her.

"Thank God for Simon, eh?" Cynthia turned to face Sally and Robert. "What a hero. You must be so proud."

"Yeah – when I'm not reaming him out for being on the mountain in the first place," Sally said, rolling her eyes. The others chuckled.

Tanya started squirming in Gwen's arms. "I'll take her to the living room," Gwen said. Finally, an escape.

She grabbed a stack of yogurt containers from a kitchen cupboard, then put Tanya on the living room floor, gingerly lowering herself down beside her. The baby happily started taking containers off the pile, handing them to Gwen, taking them back and making new stacks, chortling each time one container slipped over another.

Listening to the baby's babbles, Gwen wasn't paying attention to the conversation in the kitchen. Then, "The cabin . . . Molly Norquist . . ." caught her ear.

She turned sharply, but she couldn't make out what Cynthia said next. Then, "Shameful . . . trouble . . ."

Tanya burbled, drowning out the rest.

Absentmindedly handing a container to Tanya, Gwen tried to make sense of what she had heard. Of course she had seen the cabin, knew that someone had burned it down.

But *Molly?* Did Molly have something to do with the fire? Did *she* burn the cabin down?

And what was Molly doing in the cabin, anyway? Gwen thought indignantly. That was *her* cabin. Molly had no right –

She heard her father's name again. Cynthia's concerned query.

"Look, Tanya," Gwen said quickly, now trying to drown out her mother's words. "Look at this!" She showed the baby how to balance one container on top of another.

"Ga!" Tanya exclaimed.

Not loud enough. "X-rays . . . MRIs . . . kidney . . . permanent damage . . ."

Gwen turned her head aside, tears rolling down her cheeks. Tanya looked puzzled. She offered Gwen a container. "Ga!"

After everyone left, Gwen retreated to her chair, returning to her window, to the steady rain falling, falling. She heard her mother tidying up in the kitchen.

I should help, she thought, but she couldn't bring herself to move.

Then she heard her mother's tread. Bridget came and sat on the windowsill, facing her.

"What is it, Mom?" *Had there been a phone call she hadn't heard?* Gwen thought, alarmed. *Something from the hospital?* "Is it Dad?"

"No, it's *you.*" She leaned forward and took Gwen's hands. "I'm worried about you, honey."

Gwen let out a breath. "I – I'm okay."

"No, you're not. You're not yourself. I can see it in your face." She touched a hand to Gwen's cheek. "You're so quiet. You're hardly eating."

Gwen's mind raced, trying to think of excuses, explanations. "Mom, I –"

Her mother pulled her to her feet and wrapped her in her arms, stroking her ragged hair. "Gwennie, my darling . . . you seem so sad."

Gwen melted into her mother's warmth. For just a moment, she thought how wonderful it would be to tell her mother everything. To let it all out.

No.

"I *am* sad . . . about Dad," Gwen said carefully.

"So am I . . ." Her mother's voice cracked. She hugged Gwen tighter.

Gwen's eyes filled. She squeezed them shut.

Her mother held her at arm's length, her eyes wet with tears. "You're a wonderful daughter, to care so much."

Oh God.

"But it's still not healthy. Maybe Dr. Chan was right. Maybe you need help."

"No!" Gwen cried. "No, Mom, I don't. Really –"

Her mother placed two fingers over Gwen's lips. She gazed at her daughter. Finally she said, "We'll give it a little longer. But I'm not letting you go on like this, Gwen."

I can't go on like this either, Gwen thought. *But what can I do? What can I do?*

———

The next day, Gwen's mom went back to Vancouver. She'd been going every few days, having Sally stay over with Gwen and Percy when she could, checking in on them when she couldn't. After her mother left, Gwen was sitting, as usual, in the living room when Percy came in. Gwen had noticed that he did this now: instead of playing soccer or building tree forts or scavenging on the beach with his friends, he stayed indoors, shadowing their mother when she was home, following Gwen around when she was away. Or he stayed in his room – doing what, Gwen didn't know. Sleeping, maybe. Or staring out the window, like she did. Whatever it was, he was quiet.

Listlessly, he ran his racing cars up and down the windowsill, moving his arms mechanically, not making the gear-grinding, engine-throttling, metal-crashing noises that usually accompanied this play. Gwen took a good look at him for the first time in days. His face was pale, the freckles standing out sharply against his white skin. There were circles under his eyes. *No wonder,* Gwen thought; lately she'd heard him crying in the night. Even from the floor below, she'd be awakened by the high-pitched sound of his little-boy sobs.

On nights when their mother was home, Gwen would lie in her bed and listen for the sound of her footsteps crossing the hallway above, the soothing murmurs, Percy's half-articulated "Daddy . . ." and "scared . . ." and "die . . . ," then the gradual hushing of his cries, the soft footfalls padding back across the hall.

Last night, though, their mother had been in Vancouver, and Gwen was awakened by Percy's muffled weeping. She lay there, rigid, knowing she should go to him, unable to move. What could she say to him? How could she comfort him? So she stayed where she was, listening to every choked sob, until his cries finally tapered into silence.

Now, he put down the cars and stood in front of Gwen.

"Gwen?"

"Hmm?"

"Do you miss Daddy?"

Gwen froze. "Yes."

"Me too. A lot." A pause. "I wish I could see him. Just . . . see him."

Gwen didn't answer. *Me too*. She longed for it. She was terrified at the thought.

Percy put his hand on Gwen's arm. "Gwen? Daddy's really bad, isn't he?"

"Yes."

He swallowed. "Gwen?"

"Yeah?"

"What if . . . what if he doesn't make it?"

Gwen threw off his hand. "Percy, for God's sake! What kind of a thing is that to say?"

"But I just want to know —"

"That's horrible!"

"But Gwen —"

"I don't want to talk about it."

"But what if —"

"Forget it!"

He stared at her, lip trembling. Then he ran upstairs.

Gwen gripped the arms of her chair, waiting for her heart to stop racing. She focused on the view. Clouds scudded across the sky like tumbling rolls of cotton. A fishing boat became a distant speck. Slowly her breathing returned to normal. She emptied her mind. No thoughts. No questions. She sat, a rock, a tree, watching the sky grow dark, watching night creep up from the horizon like a curtain being drawn upward from the edge of the earth.

EIGHT

I pound on the door. I'm supposed to meet Cal here so we can talk to Bridget and find out what she wants me to do. But I've come early, on purpose, to have it out with Gwen.

No one answers. I pound again, harder. Finally the door opens. Gwen stares at me. I don't let her say a word. "You ratted on me!" I yell, stepping inside.

"What?"

"You ratted me out! Called the cops and got me in trouble."

Only it turns out I was wrong. It couldn't have been her, because she was in the hospital at the time. She had been with her dad in that avalanche. How was I supposed to know?

I turn away and Gwen closes the door. Of course I feel like an ass. She looked devastated to be accused. But there's more to it than that, I think. She seems . . . weird. Not quite there. Haggard. And what's up with that crazy, ragged haircut? I guess being in an avalanche can really mess you up.

Now what? Cal isn't here yet. I figure I'll wait for him on the porch. Just as I go to sit down on a chair, Bridget comes out of the kitchen and sees me.

"Molly!" she says. "Oh, Molly, what have you done?" Only she doesn't say it harshly, like my mom; she says it as if her heart's breaking. As if she had such hopes for me, and I've totally let her down.

"I'm sorry, Bridget," I say, my voice thick. "I'm so sorry."

She takes two steps toward me and wraps me in her arms. How can she hug me? I hug her back, fighting tears. She steps away, holding me by the shoulders. "You crazy girl! How could you be so stupid? You knew that stove was old and rickety." Before I can answer, she says, "I'm just so glad you're all right. You could have been killed!"

I can't believe this. It makes me feel worse. I wish she was mad. I wish she'd yell and scream and let me have it.

I deserve it. Walking here today, I couldn't avoid going by the cabin. It's nothing but a pile of ash and scorched earth, a few half-burned boards scattered like oversize matchsticks. The woodstove, its chimney toppled over, stands in the middle of the cold ashes like a wrecked ship. There's a smell of old, wet charcoal, like when you douse a campfire.

I didn't want to look, but I had to. I wanted to turn back the clock. I wanted to dig a hole and disappear into it.

Now, Bridget shakes her head. "What's happened to you, Molly?"

I don't know if she means *Where have you been?* or *What have you turned into?* I pretend she means the first. "Oh, I've been around . . . you know . . . hanging out . . ."

She gives me a look. I'm not fooling her. "I don't hear good things."

I look away. "Does Andrew know?" I ask in a low voice.

She gives a strangled laugh. "Andrew? No. Andrew's mostly been unconscious. On top of that, Gwen thinks she's injured. Percy's a mess. And I . . ." She runs a hand through her wavy black hair. She doesn't finish. She doesn't have to. There've always been lines in her face, vertical lines down her cheeks, horizontal lines in her forehead – but now they're deeper. There are dark shadows under her eyes. She looks old.

We stand there. I don't know what to say. Just then a car door slams. Cal lumbers over. There's an awkward moment when he looks at her. He starts to put out his hand, then reaches out and hugs her instead. "Bridget, I'm so sorry about Andrew. How is he doing?"

She tells him. He pats her shoulder, looking embarrassed. Then he looks at me and clears his throat.

"All right, we all know why we're here, so we'd better get on with it," Cal says, and he explains how things are going to work. I'm to report to Bridget's every weekday after school. He gives Bridget a form to keep track of when I come, when I leave, and what work I do. He won't come with me every time, but he'll pop in once in a while to make sure I'm doing what I'm supposed to. When I've completed the thirty hours, Bridget will sign the form and my community work service will be over.

"One more thing," he says, glancing from me to Bridget, his cheeks coloring a little. "Just because we're neighbors doesn't mean we can cut corners. Everything has to be done right. Is that clear?"

"Yes," I say.

"Yes," Bridget says.

"Good. Just needed to get that out of the way." His cheeks color more. I actually feel sorry for him. It can't be easy having to enforce the law with people you've known all your life. "So, Bridget, what would you like Molly to do today?"

She shrugs. "God, I don't know. There's a million things that need doing. How about if she starts by bringing in firewood? And splits a basket of kindling? Is that the kind of thing I'm supposed to give her?"

"Whatever you like."

"Okay. That'll be good for today."

Cal nods. "All right, I'll leave you to it. Don't forget to keep up with that form. And Molly, if Bridget's not here, you can enter the information yourself. I think we can trust her to do that, don't you, Bridget?"

She stares at me. "Absolutely."

My eyes fill again.

Cal motions for me to walk him to his car. He glances at me, then at his shoes. "Word's going around that you weren't alone in the cabin, Molly. You don't have to take this punishment alone."

I feel my cheeks flame. "It was just me."

"That's hard to believe."

I don't answer.

He sighs. "All right, if that's the way you want it. But listen, Molly. This can be a new beginning for you. Get yourself straightened out. Do your service and start over. We're . . . uh . . . we're all pulling for you."

My throat clenches. He looks at me, gets in his car, and drives away.

I head for the woodshed. From behind I hear a shout of "Molly!" and a little boy barrels into me.

"Percy!"

He throws his arms around me. Then, as if realizing what he's doing, he lets me go. Looking embarrassed, he says, "I've missed you."

"I've missed you too."

"You have?" His freckled face lights up. Then he frowns. "Then how come you don't come over anymore?"

"Oh, well . . . you know how it is . . . things change."

And not just between me and Gwen, I think. Percy's changed too. Gotten taller, leaner. At nine, he's less of a little boy. But it's more than that. He also looks drawn, unhappy. *Percy's a mess,* Bridget had said. Poor kid.

"Did you really burn down the cabin?" he asks, following me into the woodshed.

"Yes."

"That's really bad."

I put a chunk of fir on the chopping block and look around for the ax. "Yes."

"But Mommy told me you have to do work for us. So at least you'll be around," he says, brightening.

I have to chuckle. "At least I will, Perce." I find the ax, give the log a whack, and it splits evenly. The resin-y smell of fir wafts out. I ready one of the half-blocks for another cut. "Do me a favor, Perce? Go get the kindling basket from the house?" I don't want to go inside.

"Sure. Be right back." He takes off. I watch him go, watch those sticking-out ears disappear down the trail.

I suppose it's always that way – you can't stand your own siblings but you love your friends'. Gwen used to think my sisters were so fascinating. She spent hours looking from one to the other to find the tiny differences: the beauty mark on Joanna's right cheek, the one on the left of Juliet's nose, the fact that Juliet's ears were set slightly higher on her head than Joanna's. Gwen loved dressing them up when they were really young: two little sailor girls with white caps and striped shirts; two little cats with sock paws and pinned-on tails.

To me, they were a total bore. The Miss Prisses. Paper dolls and coloring in the lines and tea parties and please and thank you. They never even cracked a smile when I made them a lemon meringue pie with shaving cream. Instead they went crying to my mom, who bawled me out.

But Percy! I think, finishing with the fir and starting on a chunk of hemlock. He was always roll and tumble and tickle and tag. Of course, Gwen didn't want anything to do with him; I had to beg to get her to let him join us in the cabin. "He'll be good. Won't you, pal?" I'd say, and Percy would promise. He'd sit rapt, his legs dangling over the edge of the stump chair, as we put on plays, giggling when I mugged at the funny parts; or he'd stand exactly where we put him, being a tree or a mountain or a door.

I continue splitting wood, remembering one time when I was sleeping over. The three of us were watching a movie, and Percy kept asking questions: "Who's that lady?" and "Why's that girl crying?" and "Why'd that man steal that other man's hat?" Gwen got so fed up she told Percy to get lost. He left the room with a loud sigh. I felt so sorry for him that I followed him upstairs, just to give him a hug. I planned to go right back down.

Instead he asked, "Want to play?"

"Sure," I said. The movie wasn't very good. Besides, Gwen wouldn't miss me for a few minutes.

Within moments, a full-pitched battle from *The Lord of the Rings* was raging in his room. It was Orcs versus Elves, and there were tiny plastic guys arranged on the dresser, on the windowsill, on the bed. I was the Orcs, of course. The bad guys. They were hideous, hunched-over creatures with plastic fangs and spiny things sticking out of their heads and curved swords gripped in their grasping little hands. The Elves were tall and graceful, with flowing robes and bows and arrows.

Percy took a handful of Elves and smashed them against the Orcs in my hand. "Take that, you evil Orcs!"

"Aah!" I said, letting the Orcs fall to the floor, mortally wounded.

I attacked, ambushing a troop of Elves from behind the bed. "Aah-eee!"

A few Elves died, but then, miraculously, the others let loose with their arrows, and the Orc platoon was decimated. Some marksmen, those Elves.

We flew around the room, scurrying around the bed, in and out of the closet, behind the door.

"Gotcha!"

"Die, you miserable creature!"

"For Erendel!"

Orcs were dropping like flies; when I acted out one particularly gruesome death, gripping my throat and making gurgling sounds as the Orc in my hand writhed back and forth before falling, facedown, on the floor. Percy laughed out loud.

Finally the last Orc died. I helped Percy clean up his room – that took a while, I can tell you; there were even guys in his shoes. Then I tucked him in and sang to him, and I guess I fell asleep because the next thing I knew Gwen was shaking me awake, saying, "Hey, I thought you were *my* friend!" But she wasn't mad.

That's how it was with Percy.

I miss him, I think now as he comes back with the kindling basket. I've got a good pile of split wood, so I start making kindling. I grab the hatchet, stand up a piece of cedar, set the hatchet blade in the top, and tap both of them on the chopping block. A slender piece of wood splits off.

As I ready the hatchet for the next cut, I glance at Percy. He's sitting on a round of wood, chin in hand, not saying anything. This isn't like him. Normally he'd be chattering away, showing me his latest scab or the crab leg he found at the beach, or kicking a soccer ball from foot to foot, or shooting chips of wood through an old basketball hoop that hangs off a corner post.

I make the next cut. The flat stick of kindling snaps off and falls to the woodshed floor.

Percy says, "Did you hear about Daddy?"

I pause. "Yes."

"He's really bad. He might have to have an operation."

"I'm sorry, Percy."

"I wish I could talk to him. So he could tell me about the avalanche."

I turn to look at him. "Why do you want to know about that?"

He shrugs. "Just so I could know." A pause. "Maybe I wouldn't miss him so much."

I have no answer for that. I split another piece of kindling.

Percy continues, "Mommy goes to Vancouver all the time. She's never home."

"So it's just you and Gwen?"

He shakes his head. "Sometimes Sally sleeps over. But not every time." He sighs. "It's lonely."

I put down the hatchet, brush off the chopping block, and motion for Percy to come. He climbs onto my lap. He's really too big now, all arms and legs, but he folds himself in and fits.

"You have Gwen," I say.

He makes a small sound of exasperation. "Gwen won't talk to me. About Daddy. Or anything."

"What do you mean?"

"She just sits there. She doesn't do anything. Just sits there and looks out the window."

What's that about? I wonder. *Gwen thinks she's injured,* Bridget had said. And she's just sitting in a chair, looking out the window? Weird. In the old days, I would've charged right in there and made her tell me what was going on. But now . . . now I can't.

Percy huddles into a tighter ball. "I want Daddy to come home," he says in a trembling voice.

He will, Percy, he'll be fine, I want to tell him. But I don't. Because it might not be true, and if there's one thing I don't want to do, it's lie. So I just hug him, hold him close for a moment.

"Come on," I say, "help me get the wood in."

I fill the basket with the kindling and hand that to Percy, then load up the wheelbarrow with chunks of split wood. We walk to the house. Bridget asks me to fill the tin bucket next to the fireplace and stack the rest on the porch.

Carrying an armful of wood, I go through the kitchen and down the hall. There's something different about the house. Empty. And not just because Andrew's not there. I can't put my finger on it.

I go into the living room. Gwen's sitting in the easy chair by the window. Her back is to me, but I can tell by the sudden stiffness in her posture that she knows I'm there. She half-turns. Our eyes meet. Her cheeks bloom pink. I feel my own face flush and I want to say *I'm sorry for accusing you,* but she looks away before I can say anything. The words die in my throat.

I dump the wood in the bucket and go out to get another armful. When I come back in, Gwen is nearly across the living room. Over her shoulder she gives me a strange look, as if she's afraid of me. Or afraid of something. Moving slowly, leaning on the cane, she turns and disappears down the hall.

I go back outside. As I pile the rest of the split wood at one end of the porch, all I can think is, *What's going on? What's she afraid of? Why'd she run away?*

Then I remind myself that it really doesn't matter. Gwen's not my friend anymore. I'm just serving my time.

NINE

Gwen heard the footsteps and immediately knew they were Molly's. How many times had she heard the kitchen door open, listened to that tread, and come flying to Molly, saying, "Hey, Moll, listen to this," then read her a funny passage from a book she was in the middle of? Or said, "Hey, Moll, watch this," and showed her a new dance she'd made up? How many times had she heard those footsteps and called, "Mom, Molly and I are going to the beach . . . to the clearing . . . to the cabin"?

She stiffened. She didn't want to face Molly, not after Molly had accused her of calling the cops – as if she would! Not after Molly had rubbed it in her face that they were no longer friends by bringing her other friends, her new friends, to the cabin. Most of all she didn't want Molly asking questions about the avalanche.

But as much as Gwen willed herself not to, she couldn't resist turning around. Right away, from the look on Molly's face, Gwen knew that Molly was sorry about what she'd said before.

As soon as Molly set down her load and left, Gwen pushed herself up and started limping across the room, heading for the bathroom, the kitchen, her temporary bedroom downstairs – anywhere.

Not quick enough. Molly was back before Gwen had made it to the doorway. Gwen felt Molly's eyes on her back as she covered the last few steps. She didn't turn around.

In her bedroom, Gwen sank onto the bed. Letting the cane fall to the floor, she covered her face with her hands.

Where had it gone wrong? Sure, there was the fight at Gwen's party, the big blowout. But it had started before that . . .

Gwen could barely remember the time before she and Molly became best friends. Gwen must have been five or six when Molly moved to Thor Falls. They were an unlikely twosome, Gwen, the thin, quiet dreamer, and Molly, the chubby, brash daredevil. Molly didn't dance. Gwen didn't play soccer. Molly didn't eat tofu. Gwen didn't talk back to her parents.

Yet from the moment Molly came up to her on the playground and said, "I'm Molly. Want to dig up snails?" something had clicked, and they were soon inseparable. They rode their bikes all over town. They finished each other's sentences. They dug up not only snails, but also sand crabs, earthworms, and some globby white bugs that turned out, disgustingly, to be termites.

The Torrances' old cabin became their hangout. At Gwen's urging, Molly would make up silly little songs: "The queen ate a watermelon . . . and had a baby called Helen . . . la-la-la, da-da-da . . ." And Gwen would dance the queen, the palace, the dragon who ate the queen up, trying out the new *pas de chat* she'd learned in Mrs. Truman's class and adding a few moves of her own.

Molly led Gwen in escapades. She'd say, "Let's find a rotten fish and throw it at the first car that goes by."

Gwen's response was always "No, we can't!"

"Come on, it'll be fun."

And with delicious trepidation, Gwen would hide with Molly in the bushes at the side of the road, breathing through her mouth to avoid the stench of the rotting salmon they'd found at the beach, and then, at the sound of car wheels, haul back and – "One, two, three!" – heave it at the approaching car and streak back through the woods, squealing with laughter. One time it turned out to be a cop car!

So it went. Sleepovers and stupid jokes and secret languages. Lost teeth and backyard camping, sleeping curled like two spoons.

Sure, there were other friends. Tall, hefty Susie, who loved to play house, with herself as the mama, petite Gwen as the delicate child, and, grudgingly, when necessary, Molly as the unruly sibling. Danny, who led scavenges on the beach and knew every seashell and barnacle, who taught them to fish, and could even gut and split their catch and roast it over a rock-ringed beach fire while Gwen and Molly picked wild blueberries for dessert.

Carley and Janelle, who joined Gwen in dancing out through the studio door after class, practicing their new dance down the sidewalk, Carley laughing at her own mistakes – "Reach left, reach right, and then what? Oh, yeah, sail turn. . . . Oops, sorry, Gwen"; and Janelle, small and sprightly, whose short brown hair framed a thin, fox-like face, and who, Gwen knew, was secretly jealous of her for being Mrs. Truman's favorite because Gwen danced with her whole being and Janelle, with her beautifully pointed feet and erect back, merely danced correctly.

Good friends, all. Good friends whom Gwen played with at the playground and invited to all her birthday parties, and who filled the space when Molly went to Vancouver to visit her grandparents. But it was always Gwen and Molly.

One day a year earlier, in the spring of grade seven, the two were strolling together at recess while Gwen told Molly about a show she'd seen, starring a scruffy, wiery-haired mutt whom no one wanted, who barked to alert everyone about a drowning child and became a hero.

"And they put up a statue of him and everything," Gwen finished. "Chester the Lifesaving –"

Molly nudged her. She nodded toward a group of boys who were roughhousing, trying to wrestle each other to the ground. Gwen looked, expecting Molly to say, "Look at those jerks." Instead Molly said, "You think Jake's cute?"

Gwen looked at her in astonishment. "Jake? Jake Tyler?"

"Yeah."

"No! I think he's stupid."

Molly giggled. It was a giggle Gwen had never heard from her before, a girlish giggle out of the movies. "Well, I think he's cute."

"Yuck!"

"Oh, come on, Gwennie, don't be a baby. We're supposed to like boys."

Gwen looked away. It was no secret that Molly was more developed than she was. Half a year older – Molly had turned thirteen already – half a head taller, she had grown breasts and started wearing a bra months before, while Gwen remained utterly flat-chested. Molly even had regular periods, and made a big deal out of it, lying with a heating pad for the cramps, retiring to the bathroom every half hour, it seemed, to change her pad.

But a crush on a boy! And not just any boy, but loud, show-offy Jake Tyler, who already had hair under his arms and who snuck up behind girls and snapped their bras – those who had them.

Gwen looked at Molly out of the corner of her eye. Molly's face was flushed, and she kept glancing at Jake as if willing him to look at her.

"I like boys," Gwen said defensively, thinking of Percy, and little Paul next door, and even Danny, who was more like a brother to her than – well, than *that*.

"Yeah, right," Molly said, rolling her eyes. "Like Percy?"

Caught, Gwen couldn't help but smile. "Well . . . yeah." She burst out laughing, and Molly laughed with her, the two of them doubling over with mirth, just like always. But there was something shrill in Molly's laughter.

A month later, on a Saturday afternoon, Molly called. "Meet me in the clearing. I've got a surprise."

Gwen hurried to the meeting place, the clearing between her lot and Sally and Simon's. A huge old cedar stump stood in the middle of it, with a flat top that had often served as their table for picnics, or as a stage on which Gwen danced, or as a perch where they sat with their legs dangling down and tried out names for their future children, two for Molly and two sets of twins for Gwen.

Molly met her with an expectant smile. She wiggled out a cough syrup bottle from her jeans pocket. Only it didn't hold cough syrup, Gwen saw, but a clear liquid.

"Check this out," Molly said, unscrewing the lid.

"What is it?"

"Gin."

"Gin!"

"Sh!" Molly glanced around.

"Where'd you get it?"

"My parents' liquor cabinet." Molly grinned.

"Do they know?"

"Of course not, you idiot. Here, try some." She held out the bottle.

Gwen shook her head. "No, thanks."

"Come on, Gwen, it's not going to kill you." Molly took a gulp herself and held out the bottle again. "Come on, it's fun."

Gwen took a small sip. It was bitter, like medicine, only without the sugar to hide the taste, and it burned going down. She coughed. "Yuck! It's gross."

Molly giggled. "Yeah, it *tastes* bad . . . but it makes you *feel* good." She drank again.

When she offered the bottle once more, Gwen shook her head. "That stuff is awful."

Molly shrugged and took another sip. "Suit yourself." She told Gwen how, the night before, her parents had had some friends over for dinner. Molly, helping to clear the table, had snuck a taste from each of the glasses.

"It made me tipsy," she said with a laugh, drinking again. The cough syrup bottle was now nearly empty. "So after my parents went to bed, I snuck downstairs and snitched some out of one of the bottles."

Her breath smelled ripe, and her eyes were beginning to glaze over.

"Come on, Gwen, have some more."

"No," Gwen said. "And I don't think you should either."

Molly looked at her blearily. "God, you're no fun."

"What, because I don't want to get drunk?"

"I'm not drunk," Molly said. "I'm just . . . fooling around."

"You look drunk to me."

"That's because you don't know what you're talking about."

"Well, count me out."

"God, you are such a wimp."

"I am not!" Gwen felt tears start to well up in her eyes.

"You are so. 'No, I shouldn't. You shouldn't.'" Molly mimicked a whiny little-girl voice.

"That's not fair."

"It's true. If you don't want to have fun –" She stopped.

"What?"

Molly flushed. "Then I'll find someone who does!" She stomped out of the clearing.

The next day, at recess, Molly hung out with Nikki – Nikki whom everyone whispered about, Nikki who apparently smoked and drank and had parties with her older brother Zach while their mother was out half the night.

Kicking a soccer ball with Susie and Carley, Gwen tried not to look at Molly's head bent close to Nikki's, the two of them veering close to the boys, calling out gibes that Gwen couldn't hear, laughing when the boys called back.

Gwen's stomach tightened. Was Nikki more fun than she was?

They made up. Of course they made up. Molly came over and they spent the whole weekend together, just the two of them, exploring on the beach and baking cookies and doing each other's hair. Just like best friends.

Little by little, though, other friends began to whisper. One day Susie said, "I saw Molly behind the store the other day. Smoking a joint."

"She was not!" Gwen said, though she had no idea if it was true.

"She was, Gwen. Her and Nikki. I smelled it."

Susie's face was a mask of concern, but Gwen saw a thin gleam of satisfaction there, too. Gwen turned away.

For the spring school dance that year, Gwen wore new denim capris and a blousy, pink, scooped-neck top. She put on dangly silver earrings, then carefully applied mascara and pink lip gloss in front of her bedroom mirror, wiping away the excess with toilet paper so she wouldn't look too made-up.

When she came downstairs, her father threw his hands in the air. "Bridget, come and see the young woman your daughter has turned into."

"Dad," Gwen said, rolling her eyes, secretly pleased.

When Gwen and her dad picked Molly up, she came out in skintight jeans and a formfitting tank top that showed the curve of her breasts and lots of midriff. Her eyes were outlined in thick black, her lashes caked in mascara.

At first, Molly hung out with Gwen, Susie, Janelle, and Carley near the refreshments table while they waited for the music to start. A group of kids fiddled with a CD player, bursts of music filling the room, then cutting out. Girls and guys huddled in separate groups, eyeing each other. A balloon fell from the basketball hoop, and up-stretched hands batted it around the room.

Molly leaned close to Gwen. "Jake looks hot, eh?"

Gwen looked to where Jake, in baggy jeans and spiked hair, lounged with his friends. "Yeah, I guess so," trying to sound like she meant it.

Molly giggled. "I'm just going over to say hi." She squeezed through the crowd.

"Why doesn't she forget about the top and just go in her bra?" Janelle said into Gwen's ear.

Gwen turned sharply. "That's my best friend you're talking about, Janelle."

Janelle blushed, darting a glance at Susie and Carley.

A moment later, Gwen saw Molly standing with Nikki, whose outfit – the tight jeans and skimpy top – was so identical that it had to have been planned. A stab of jealousy pricked her. Why had Molly coordinated her outfit with Nikki, and not with her?

Gwen danced with Danny, who looked ill at ease with his hair slicked back. Once she caught him staring at her with such an odd expression that she wondered if he felt all right, and then thought maybe it was – Could it be? Her old buddy Danny? – and felt so funny that she nearly stumbled. She danced in a mob with her girlfriends, and then with Danny again, and drank more soda and ate more chips than she had in a year.

Although Gwen tried not to look for Molly, her eyes couldn't help seeking her out. All evening Molly hung out with Nikki. They whispered, checked their makeup in small mirrors, shimmied to the fast songs, slow-danced with Jake and his pals. Once Gwen saw Molly and Nikki slip out the gym doors and briefly join a group of older kids outside. When they came back in, they were shrieking with laughter.

Not once did Molly turn and look for Gwen.

Finally the dance ended. Knots of kids left in twos and threes, calling goodnight. Parents' cars drove slowly away, red taillights disappearing down the street.

Molly drifted back to where Gwen was leaning against the gym wall. Molly's face was flushed, her eye makeup smudged.

Gwen folded her arms, determined not to say anything, willing her father to come.

"Sorry," Molly mumbled.

"What?"

"I . . . sort of ditched you."

Gwen tried not to picture Molly on the opposite side of the gym, spending the night with Nikki. "You can hang out with whoever you want, Molly."

"I just wanted to have fun." Molly sounded defensive.

Gwen didn't answer. Molly took several steps closer. Gwen sniffed. "God, Molly, have you been smoking pot?"

"So what if I have?"

Gwen shook her head. So Susie had been right. She, Gwen, hadn't wanted to believe it – not that Molly had tried it; Gwen knew that most kids did – but that she was doing it a lot, and brazenly. With Nikki.

"You better watch it, Molly."

"Oh, don't be such a prude."

"That's not what I meant."

Molly took a step closer. "Why don't you just butt out, Gwen?"

"What?"

"If you don't want to have fun, that's your business. But don't tell me what to do!"

"I wasn't –"

"You act like it's so terrible and you're so perfect."

"I do not! I don't think you're terrible. I just don't want you to get in trouble."

Molly scowled. "The only way I'm getting in trouble is if you tell on me."

"I'd never do that!"

They stared at one another. Gwen felt her cheeks flame.

Molly gave an awkward smile. "What are we fighting about?"

Gwen forced a chuckle. "Are we fighting?"

"I hope not."

"Me too."

They both laughed as Andrew's truck pulled up.

"Sorry I'm late," he said. "How was the dance?"

"Fine," both girls said.

They didn't say another word all the way home.

It was at Gwen's thirteenth birthday party that it all fell apart. She was having a sleepover – Molly, Susie, Carley, Janelle, plus a couple of other girls. They were going to make mini pizzas, eat birthday cake, open presents, and – grand surprise – do karaoke with a machine her parents had rented in Norse River.

Molly came over early to help Gwen move furniture. They carried the coffee table to the corner, pushed the easy chair aside, then moved the couch, grunting with each heave, laughing at the mystery objects that showed up beneath it: two of Percy's Orcs, which, although he wouldn't admit it, he still played with from time to time; a library book due a year ago; a picture of Gwen and Molly at about age seven, arms around each other, grinning gap-toothed smiles.

"Remember that? We both lost teeth eating corn on the cob," Gwen said, blowing dust off the picture.

Molly nodded. "My cob got all bloody. Yuck!"

They laughed.

When they'd shoved the couch against the living room wall, Molly gestured at the buffet next to it.

"Hey, Gwennie, look at that."

"What?"

"That." Molly pointed to a cluster of liquor bottles standing on a shelf.

Gwen looked. There were a couple of bottles of wine; a squat, curvy one filled with Irish cream, and a tall, rectangular one of vodka.

An uneasy feeling prickled Gwen's insides. "What about it?"

Molly leaned close. "What do you say we snitch a little from each? For later?"

Gwen smiled at her. "You're kidding, right?"

"Come on, it'll be fun. Give our karaoke a bit of a kick." Giggling, holding an imaginary mic to her lips, she shook her hips like a rock star.

Gwen stared at her. "You'd steal from my parents?"

Molly's smile faded. "Oh, come on, Gwen, we'll just take a little. They'll never know."

Something dropped in Gwen's stomach. "I can't believe you said that."

"It's no big deal. Everybody does it."

"Not me! Maybe your new friends do, but not me."

"No kidding," Molly said in a sour voice. "You don't do anything."

"What's that supposed to mean?"

"You're no fun anymore."

Gwen's face felt warm. "Because I won't steal booze from my parents?"

"Give me a break. You make it sound like a crime."

"It's wrong!"

Molly rolled her eyes. "You're such a goody-goody, Gwen."

"I am not!"

"You are so."

"You think it's so cool to drink and get high, but it's not, it's stupid —"

"How would you know? You never try it. It's boring . . ." Molly trailed off.

"Boring being with me?"

"Yeah!"

"Then why don't you go hang out with your cool friends? I'm sure *they're* not boring."

"You better believe it."

"Then go."

"Okay, I will."

"And don't come back!"

"I won't!"

She left, slamming the door.

Somehow, Gwen got through the party. When her friends asked where Molly was, she said, "Oh . . . she got sick all of a sudden."

"Really?" Janelle sounded skeptical.

Gwen oohed and aahed over her birthday presents and even forced herself to sing "Y.M.C.A." with the others, doing all the movements and laughing along.

The next morning, after everyone left, she climbed back into bed and cried.

All that summer, Gwen waited for Molly to call, to come flying over on her bike, to apologize.

She didn't.

Several times she saw Molly in a throng of other kids, at the beach, at the store.

She turned away.

One day Percy asked, "Where's Molly? I miss her."

Gwen turned on him. "She wasn't *your* friend!"

Percy staggered back a step. "I was just asking."

"I don't know. And I don't care!"

Now, sitting on her bed with her arms wrapped around her knees, Gwen thought bitterly that she'd finally gotten her wish. Molly was back. Only now Gwen didn't want her here. And for sure Molly didn't want to be here. They had nothing to say to each other. It was beyond awkward, it was humiliating.

Gwen lay down and clutched her pillow to her middle. She was just going to have to stay out of Molly's way, that was all. She'd disappear into her room when Molly came. Take a bath. Take a nap. Become engrossed in some stupid TV show.

It shouldn't be too hard to avoid Molly, Gwen thought glumly. Molly didn't want anything to do with her either.

TEN

Every day I do my community work service. Prune the flower beds. Paint the trim on the porch. Dig the garden. Bridget's form starts filling up. Every few days Cal comes to check up on me. Bridget tells him I'm doing what I'm supposed to, and he nods and says, "Good." He looks like he's hiding a smile. Like he's rooting for me.

He checks in with my parents. They tell him I've been sober. That I'm obeying my nine o'clock curfew. As if I have any choice. They practically guard the door to my room.

Cal fills out more forms.

My thirty hours count down, one by one.

School starts again after spring break. I don't want to go back. I don't want to see my friends. I don't know what to say to them, or what they're going to say to me.

They haven't called. Or e-mailed. Or texted. I haven't seen any of them since the arrest.

At first I expected them to come forward and admit that they were responsible too. It didn't happen. And I realized that that wasn't realistic. I mean, would I voluntarily turn myself in and say, "Hey, I'm guilty, punish me too?" Well, yeah, I would. But you can't expect people to do that. Besides, I knew that Tony and Zach had already gotten in trouble with the cops, so getting nailed again would definitely be bad news for them.

So then I expected them to call. Say they were sorry for how things turned out. Thank me for keeping my mouth shut.

That didn't happen either.

Now, as I walk into school, I don't know what to think. I still can't believe they meant to shaft me. We were too tight, having too much fun. Have they been afraid my parents might intercept their calls and find out who they are? Are they just lying low until I finish my community work service, and the cops and courts are out of the picture, and then they'll come back and we'll pick up where we left off?

I don't know.

I walk into homeroom, and the first thing I see is that Nikki's hanging with this girl Teresa. Teresa has a dragon tattoo on her ankle and chemically straightened hair. She's also got an older brother who can score booze, and a family cabin in the mountains.

They've pushed their desks together and are laughing at something on Teresa's cell phone.

I go over and stand beside Nikki's desk. She looks up. Turns pink. "Hey," she mumbles, not looking me in the eye.

I wait. When she doesn't say anything else, I blurt stupidly, "How was your break?"

"Fine," she says.

I wait for her to ask me about mine. To ask me how I've been. To ask about what I've been going through.

Teresa nudges her and, giggling, says, "Check this out." Nikki bends over the cell phone again.

I stand there like an idiot, then walk to my desk.

Between classes, I spot Zach down the hall in a throng of guys coming toward me. I lift my hand to wave. I think he sees me, but he ducks into a classroom before I reach him.

At lunch I see Crystal. She gives me her blissed-out smile, but she doesn't come over.

At the end of the day, I come upon the group of them, hanging in front of Tony's locker. Tony, Zach, Gretchen, Crystal, Nikki – and Teresa.

I stand in front of them. They dart glances at one another, at me, away again. Tony puts in one book, takes out another. Gretchen checks her nails. Finally Zach smiles and asks, "How's it going?"

"How's it going!" I shout.

Tony glances up and down the hall. "Chill, Molly. Don't make a scene."

That's exactly what I want to do, but I grit my teeth. "I'm not."

There's a silence, a lot of shifting from foot to foot. Eventually Nikki says, "We thought you were with us, Molly."

"Yeah, we thought you were right behind us," Gretchen adds.

"We told you to come," Zach says.

"Yeah . . . that's right . . . we did . . ." the others chime in.

That's true. They did. Remembering makes me feel a little better. They must have been freaked out when they regrouped and realized I wasn't there.

"So . . . we heard you got community work service," Tony says in a low voice.

That makes me pissed off again. If they'd come forward, I wouldn't have been the only one. They'd be doing it with me.

But I just nod.

"Rough, eh?" Crystal says.

At least she's asking, I think. "It's not so bad," I say, surprised to realize it's true. I don't mind doing stuff for Bridget. It's the least I can do. And I've been feeling pretty good. Turns out I don't miss the booze and pot all that much.

"You almost done?" Tony asks.

"About halfway."

"Cool," he says. "Then you'll be free, eh?"

I nod again.

Another silence falls. Then Zach zips up his jacket. "Well . . . got to go."

"Me too."

"Me too."

"See you."

Before I know it, they've all gone, passing down the hall in a tight knot.

I stand there. My stomach drops. No one said, *Sorry.* No one said, *We should have stayed.* No one said, *Come with us.*

But then, as I gather my books from my locker and walk out the door, headed for Gwen's and today's chores, I think about what Tony asked. *You almost done? . . . Then you'll be free?*

Maybe he meant, *Then you'll be free to hang out with us again. Then you'll be free to party. Then it'll go back to the way it was.*

Yes, I tell myself, my step lightening. That must be what he meant.

"Surprise!"

Gwen stood at the open front door. On the doorstep was a beaming Susie, flanked by Carley and Janelle. Susie was holding a plastic container.

"We came to cheer you up," Carley said.

"And tell you all the latest," Janelle said.

"And feed you," Susie added with a grin. Stepping inside, she lifted the lid of the container. Chocolate brownies were stacked in rows, their frosting softly gleaming.

Gwen smiled faintly. The last thing she felt like was a visit, small talk, pity, questions. All she wanted was to be left alone, to sit in her chair and watch the clouds slowly drift by.

But she motioned them into the living room, even turned

her chair around to face the room. Carley and Janelle sat on the couch, while Susie went into the kitchen to find plates and glasses.

"So, how are you feeling, Gwen?" Carley asked.

A pause. "About the same."

"Are you coming back to school?" Janelle asked.

Another pause. "Not yet."

There was a short silence, broken by the sound of Susie clattering in the kitchen.

"How's your dad?" Carley asked.

Gwen felt the quick sting of tears. She blinked rapidly. "Uh . . . not so good."

"Well, I'm sure he'll be fine, Gwen, don't worry." Carley leaned forward and patted her knee.

Gwen stiffened.

Susie bustled in, carrying a tray loaded with glasses of milk and plates of brownies. "Good thing I know my way around your kitchen, Gwen," she said with a chuckle. She set the tray on the coffee table and started handing around plates. "Eat up, Gwen, you need it." She patted her belly. "Looks like the pounds you've lost ended up on me," she said, laughing. She lifted her brownie. "I shouldn't . . . but what the hell." She bit in.

Carley licked her lips. "Delicious, Suze."

Janelle nodded, daintily lifting crumbs with her fingertip and licking them off. "You make the best brownies, Susie."

"And cookies. And cakes," Carley added, taking another bite. Susie beamed. She looked at Gwen.

Gwen quickly picked up her brownie and took a bite. "Yummy," she said. And it was – full of dark, chocolaty flavor. Trouble was, she wasn't hungry. She moved the brownie around on her plate, hoping Susie wouldn't notice.

"So, Gwen, you should have seen what happened in gym today," Carley said with a giggle, and she launched into a story about how they'd been playing volleyball, girls against boys.

"Jake, of course, was boasting about how the boys were going to kill us," Janelle said.

"And the game was really close, going back and forth, them getting a point, us getting a point," Susie said.

"And finally it was game point, and Jake spiked the ball," Carley continued.

"And it bounced off my head –" Susie said, starting to giggle. "Like, I had no idea it was coming. I was just standing there, and whomp!"

"And it bounced back over the net, right to Jake, and he was so stunned he just stood there, and it dropped – and we won the game!" Carley finished. All three girls burst out laughing.

Gwen forced a smile. "That's great."

"It was so funny."

"I bet."

A silence fell. Through the open window, from outside, there came a faint scratching sound, repeated over and over.

"What's that?" Susie asked.

"Uh . . . it's Molly. She's raking," Gwen said.

"Raking?" Carley said.

"It's her community work service," Gwen explained, feeling uncomfortable. "What she has to do to . . . you know, pay us back for the cabin."

"Oh, yeah, I heard that was the sentence," Susie said.

"It was the talk of school," Carley said.

"Not enough punishment, if you ask me," Janelle said.

"Janelle, keep it down," Gwen said. Even though she herself was furious with Molly, she didn't want her old friend to hear people say such things about her.

"Well, I don't care," Janelle said with a toss of the head. "That was a terrible thing she did – and to *you!*"

The scratching noise drew closer.

"And that story about no one else being there – that has to be a lie," Susie said.

"It does sound strange," Carley agreed.

"I just feel sorry for you, having to have her around all the time," Janelle said. "I mean, the two of you were such good friends, and now –"

The scratching of the rake was directly outside the open living room window. Gwen twisted. Because of the slope of the yard, only the top of Molly's head was visible. For a moment she looked up. Gwen's eyes locked with hers. Then Molly turned away, and Gwen turned back to the room. Her cheeks burned, though she didn't know why. Molly had betrayed *her*, so why should she feel humiliated for Molly?

The raking sound resumed, moving slowly past the window.

"So, Gwen, when are you coming back to dance class?" Janelle asked.

"Yeah, we miss you," Carley said. "I keep messing up. I need you to remind me what to do." She smiled.

"Mrs. Truman keeps calling on *me* to demonstrate." Janelle rolled her eyes, as if she minded.

Automatically Gwen reached for her cane. She gripped it in both hands. "It's not *when*. It's *if*."

"What do you mean?" Carley asked.

"My leg still hurts. It's not getting any better."

"But we heard you were okay." Susie looked puzzled. "Not hurt at all."

"That's what the doctor said. What the X-rays and MRI showed. No injury. Nothing."

"Well, if nothing showed up, it can't be that bad, right?" Carley said.

Gwen didn't answer.

Susie gave her a sympathetic look. "Whatever it is, it'll probably get better soon."

Gwen shook her head. "I can't dance on this leg." She forced herself to go on. "I don't know if I can dance anymore."

There was a stunned silence. In the quiet, Gwen realized that she didn't hear the rake. In the next moment, the scratching resumed, and Carley blurted, "But Gwen! You can't stop danc-ing! That would be so terrible!"

"Carley!" Susie scolded, glancing at Gwen.

Carley's face turned red. "Sorry, Gwen, I didn't mean –"

"It's probably just a muscle tear," Janelle interrupted. "I remember when I tore my hamstring – I was doing the splits and went too far. Aah, that hurt! I had to do icing and physio and stretching for months, and it took forever to get better. But it finally did. And it's fine now." She wagged her finger. "But you can't just sit around, Gwen. That's the worst thing. Then you get scar tissue, and then it might really not get better –"

Gwen's eyes filled.

"Janelle!" Susie snapped. "Can't you see you're making her feel worse?"

"Sorry," Janelle muttered. "I was just trying to help."

Susie got up and, leaning over, hugged Gwen. Gwen could feel the press of Susie's shoulder against her face, could smell chocolate and a fruity shampoo. She sat rigid, wishing Susie would let go.

Finally she did. She walked over to the coffee table and held up the tray. "Another brownie, anybody? There's loads. Janelle? Gwen, you haven't even eaten yours."

Gwen looked guiltily at her half-eaten brownie. "I will, Susie. Really. And you could leave some for Percy. He'd love that."

"Okay," Susie said, and went off to the kitchen to clean up. Carley and Janelle cleared the plates and glasses.

Soon after, the three girls came back into the living room to say good-bye. Giving Gwen another hug, Susie whispered, "You'll be fine, Gwen. You'll see. Everything's going to be fine."

No, it won't! Gwen wanted to shout. *You don't know anything about it, so why don't you just shut up?*

Immediately she felt ashamed. Susie was just trying to be kind. They all were. It was just — it was just that she couldn't stand it. What was wrong with her, that she couldn't let her friends be nice? That she couldn't wait until they left?

She forced herself to say, "I know. Thanks."

As soon as they were gone, she turned her chair back to face the window. She fell into it, letting her gaze drift to the far, flat horizon. Letting her mind go blank.

I hang up the rake in the toolshed. Then I push the wheelbarrow to one of the piles of leaves and twigs and dead grass. I load in the debris and dump it on the compost pile near the edge of the property.

As I head back to the house to pick up the next pile, Susie, Carley, and Janelle come out. My first thought is to hide. I hear Janelle's words in my head. *Not enough punishment . . . I feel sorry for you, having to have her around.* I imagine the self-righteous look she probably had on her pointy little face when she said that.

Forget hiding.

"Hey, girls." I flutter my fingers in greeting.

They turn. Their faces turn red. Especially Janelle's.

"Just doing my punishment here," I say cheerfully.

Janelle looks mortified. Good.

"Uh . . . hi, Molly, how's it going?" Carley asks. At least she has the decency to talk to me.

"Just great, thanks."

I roll past them to the next pile. I don't know what I'm trying to prove. They think I'm shameful, just like everybody else in Thor Falls. Showing them up isn't going to change that. But it makes me feel better, letting them know I heard. Keeps things real.

I tune out their nervous whispers. I don't even turn around as they walk away.

Then I think about what else I heard.

I don't know if I can dance anymore.

What the hell is that about? Gwen doesn't look hurt that bad to me. Granted, I haven't gotten close enough to her to really see, and she *is* using a cane. But I can't believe she's injured so badly that she'd have to stop dancing.

And that idiot, Susie, telling her everything was going be okay. What kind of bullshit is that? If Gwen had to give up dancing, nothing would be okay ever again.

Gwen stop dancing. The thought sends a chill down my back. She couldn't. She'd die.

I know it's none of my business, but I go inside anyway, into the living room. Gwen is sitting in her usual position, staring out the window. She doesn't turn, but I know she knows I'm there. I wait.

Finally she turns. "What?"

"Did you mean it?"

"Did I mean what?"

"That you couldn't dance?"

She turns pale. "What do you care?"

"I don't know, I just –"

"Butt out, Molly."

"But Gwen –"

"Butt. Out."

I don't need to be told again. I go outside. I scoop up the rest of the piles and cart them away, slamming the wheelbarrow into the wooden boards framing the compost pile.

ELEVEN

It had been two weeks since the avalanche. Gwen knew because, although she tried to block out the memory, a calendar in her head marked off the days. Two weeks since her father had been hurt. Two weeks since she had spoken to him. Two weeks of using a cane and trying not to think about Dancemakers.

Today it was raining. Gwen sat in her chair and watched it come down. It wasn't one of those dramatic storms but rather a steady, unrelenting rain, the stream of drops so fine that you couldn't be sure it was raining at all – except for the trickles of water rolling off the shiny salal leaves.

She heard a car roll up on the gravel, a car door slam, then a tap on the kitchen door. Her mother was in there – she had returned from Vancouver the day before; Gwen's father had had his spleen out; the doctors were still doing tests to see if he was going to have to lose a kidney as well – so Gwen let her answer it. There was the murmur of voices. Gwen couldn't make out who it was. Probably another neighbor with a pot of soup.

A moment later a familiar voice called out, "Gwen?"

She turned. "Mrs. Truman!" Heat flooded into her cheeks. This was the visit she'd been dreading.

Mrs. Truman hurried over. She gathered Gwen in her arms. "Oh, Gwen, my dear!"

Gwen resisted for a moment, but then gave herself over to the hug.

"How I've missed you!" Mrs. Truman said.

Not as much as I've missed you, Gwen thought, tears stinging her eyes.

Mrs. Truman helped Gwen turn her chair, then pulled up a chair to face hers. As they moved the easy chair, the cane clattered to the floor.

Mrs. Truman handed it to her. "So you're still using that?"

Gwen nodded.

"Is your leg any better?"

"Not really."

Mrs. Truman leaned forward. "What is it, Gwen? Do you know what the matter is?"

Gwen shook her head. "No one knows. It doesn't show up on any tests. It just hurts."

"Do you mind if I have a look?"

When Gwen shook her head, Mrs. Truman knelt beside her. Gwen pulled up her pant leg, and her teacher started gently feeling her leg, beginning at the ankle and working up.

Gwen looked down at the top of Mrs. Truman's head, at her

frizzy black hair escaping from the ponytail, and marveled, as she always did, at her carriage. There was something so solid, so strong, in the way Mrs. Truman held herself. Even now, in this awkward position, kneeling on the floor and twisting her head to look up at Gwen, down at her leg, up and down, her back was straight, her neck long.

A strong core, dancers called it. Yet Mrs. Truman was graceful, too, and limber, and she danced with such passion that it made Gwen want to climb inside her body and be carried along.

Twice a week she saw Mrs. Truman dance in class as she demonstrated movements and combinations, taught choreography, or showed her students the quality she wanted: an elastic fluidity, one movement bouncing into the next; or a strong jazz hand with fingers spread; or the surrender of a head giving in to gravity and pulling the torso into a downward swing.

And she had a lovely, evocative way of using vocal sounds to convey what she wanted, too. "Unh!" she'd say, going into a contraction. Or "ba-da-da-laaaa . . ." to show the quality of a quick *pas de bourrée* followed by a wide lunge to second position.

Carley always laughed at these funny sounds, and Janelle rolled her eyes as if it was mortifying to have a dance teacher who spoke gibberish. But Gwen knew exactly what Mrs. Truman meant. "Unh" *was* a contraction. "Ba-da-da" *was* the rhythm of a *pas de bourrée*. She loved the imaginativeness of the language Mrs. Truman used, the way she nailed the feeling she wanted with both body and voice.

But all of these – the short bursts when Mrs. Truman demonstrated dance moves to the class, accompanied by her made-up sounds – were only snippets. Gwen had wanted to see her *dance*. She'd gotten her wish the year before.

Mrs. Truman had invited several friends to perform with her at the arts center in Norse River. They came from Vancouver, Seattle, Banff. They had all done their graduate school training together, and they revived some of the dances they'd learned there.

The other dancers – three women and two men – were gifted, but it was Mrs. Truman whom Gwen couldn't take her eyes from. Of course she danced beautifully, finishing her pirouettes in exactly the right spot, landing her leaps with barely a sound, but it was more than that. With every stretched arm, the movement seemed to go on beyond her fingertips. Every contraction was a complete rounding of her back, a hollowing out of her front. Every rise was suspended . . . suspended . . . until, at the last possible moment, it fell into the next movement. She gave herself over completely to the dance. She *was* the dance.

Gwen remembered being transfixed. She remembered thinking, *That's exactly how I want to dance.*

But now . . .

Mrs. Truman completed her examination and stood up. "I'm mystified, Gwen. I don't see or feel anything. Will you try a few things with me?"

"Sure." She pushed herself up.

Mrs. Truman nodded. "Do a *plié*."

Gwen stood in first position and bent her knees. "Ow."

"That hurts?"

"Yeah."

"How about in parallel?"

Gwen turned her feet in and repeated the movement. "That too."

Mrs. Truman shook her head. "Try a *relevé*."

Gwen rose onto her toes. She wobbled and fell toward the left. Mrs. Truman caught her.

"Whoa! It hurts just to rise? Are you sure?"

"Yes!"

"Just on the right?"

"Yes."

"How about *tendu?* Do it with me. And out, two, three, four —"

Gwen started extending her right foot forward along the floor. She stopped partway. "I can't."

"Come on, Gwen, it's just a little *tendu*."

"I can't! It hurts! Why doesn't anybody believe me?"

She threw herself back in her chair and covered her face with her hands. There was a silence. She felt Mrs. Truman's hand on her knee. Gwen lowered her hands.

"I'm sorry, Gwen. I do believe you. It's just that it's so strange. There's no explanation."

Gwen shrugged.

"It must be so frustrating," Mrs. Truman said.

"It is."

"So, what have you tried? Ice? Heat?"

Gwen shook her head.

"Physio? Massage?"

Another shake.

"Nothing? But Gwen, you can't just sit around. You must try something. I can recommend a good physiotherapist. She's done wonders for me, and I'm sure –"

"It won't help," Gwen said in a low voice.

"Nonsense. There's plenty you can do to help yourself heal. And we've got to get you back. The year-end recital is coming up, the Dancemakers deadline is only a few weeks away –"

"I'm not applying."

"What!"

Tears stung. "Mrs. Truman, I can't dance."

Mrs. Truman gave her a piercing look. "This isn't like you, Gwen. You – of all people – to just sit there and say 'I can't'! The Gwen I know would be working like the devil to get better, not giving up."

Gwen pounded her fists on her thighs. "I don't care. I can't dance! I'm weak. I fall over – you saw! Whatever I do, it hurts. It's no use!"

There was a silence. Mrs. Truman looked at her for a long moment. Then she said gently, "Gwen . . . your mom told me what the doctor said . . . about stress . . ."

"I'm not making it up!"

"I didn't say you were. But I can see that you're down. Maybe it would be good for you to talk to someone."

"No!"

"But you could get help –"

Gwen shook her head.

"Counseling, support –"

"No."

Mrs. Truman regarded her. She seemed about to say something else, but checked herself. Instead she leaned forward and kissed Gwen on the cheek. "All right, then. Feel better, sweetheart."

She left.

Gwen turned back to the window, hooked the cane over the arm of her chair, settled back into the cushion. She heard the murmur of Mrs. Truman and her mother talking, no doubt discussing what a mess she was, trying to figure out what to do about her. She heard the door open and close, the car start up and drive away.

It was still raining.

TWELVE

A few days after Gwen told me to butt out, I show up for my work stint. I'm still pissed off. I just won't talk to her, that's all. She'll bloody well get her wish.

Today is another of Cal's checkup days. When he arrives, we go into the kitchen. Bridget shows him the form, line after line filled out, hour after hour piling up. I realize with surprise that I'm almost done.

"Molly's doing an excellent job," Bridget tells him. "She shows up on time and does whatever I ask her."

Cal initials the form. "Excellent. Great work, Molly. I knew you could keep it together." He grins at me, patting me on the back.

Despite myself, I grin back. Feels good. Even my parents have been telling me they're proud of me lately.

Bridget and I walk him outside and he leaves. I turn to her. "So, what do you want me to do today?"

She scans the grounds. "I don't know, Molly. You've pretty

much done everything. Split firewood, raked the yard, dug the garden, pruned the flower beds."

I follow her gaze. Wow. It's true. The place looks pretty damn good, if I do say so myself.

"So . . . ?"

Bridget shrugs. She looks exhausted, like she hasn't slept in days. "The house is a mess. Would it be too demeaning to ask you to vacuum?"

Demeaning? After what I've done to her? "Sure, no problem."

"Thanks. I've got to run to the grocery store. You know where everything is, right?"

Better than in my own house, I think, heading for the hall closet where they keep the vacuum cleaner. Funny how, if my mom asked me to vacuum, I'd be pissed, but when someone else asks me, I don't mind.

I'm in the hallway when I hear voices coming from the living room. Gwen and Percy. They don't seem to know I'm there.

I can't help myself. I stop and listen.

"Gwen?" Percy says.

"Yeah?"

"What was it like?"

"What was what like?"

"You know . . . up there. What did it look like?"

"Percy!" Gwen sounds alarmed.

"Could you see it coming?"

"I don't want to talk about it."

"But –"

"No."

"Was Daddy scared?"

"Stop it!"

"Gwen, please. I need to know . . . about Daddy."

No answer.

"Gwen?" Percy says again.

"What?"

"Would you take me up there?"

"Up where?"

"Mount Odin. To see where it happened."

"*What!*"

I have the same reaction. Take Percy up to where the avalanche came down? What kind of crazy question is that?

"Please?" Percy says.

"Are you out of your mind?"

"But I just want to *see*, Gwen."

"No way!"

"I really want to go –"

"Drop it, Percy."

"Then I'll go myself!"

"You're not allowed, and you know it –"

"I don't care."

"You're not going and that's that."

"I hate you!" I hear Percy's footsteps running out of the living room, up the stairs.

Whoa, I think. Of all the wild requests. Where did that come from? Then I remember the conversation I had with Percy, when he said he missed Andrew so much. Maybe seeing the avalanche site would make him feel closer to his dad. Less lonely.

Still, I don't blame Gwen for saying no. It would be brutal for her to have to go back up there. And with her leg it would be a hard climb.

That makes me wonder about the avalanche. What *was* it like? What does the mountain look like now? Is the area still covered with snow? Or is it bare and scraped raw?

I try to picture where the snow would have come down, but I can't get a clear image. I haven't been on Mount Odin in a long time, I realize – since I hiked up with Gwen's family a couple of years ago. In a way it would be cool to go up and check it out. See what nature unleashed looks like.

Then I bring myself back to earth, right down to ground level. I've got work to do, and I'd better get on with it.

I haul out the vacuum cleaner. As I clunk past the living room, I see Gwen sitting in her chair. She doesn't turn, although I know she knows I'm there. The cane is hooked over the arm of the chair. So she's still using it. *Her leg must hurt pretty bad,* I think.

Then I catch myself. I'm butting out, remember?

But as I continue down the hall, I can't help but feel that there's something weird about the whole thing. Something weird about *her.* All she does is sit and brood. Sure, I know she's bummed out and all, but something doesn't fit. I don't know what. I've just got this feeling.

Again, I tell myself to forget about it.

I carry the vacuum upstairs, clean the hallway and the upstairs bathroom – Bridget's right, there are dust balls everywhere – then nudge open the door of Percy's room. He's sitting on his bed, cross-legged, staring into space.

"Molly!" he says, brightening.

I shut off the vacuum and sit next to him. If anything, he looks worse than he did last time. His face looks pinched, and the circles under his eyes are even darker. There are a few Orcs and Elves lying on the quilt, but he isn't playing with them.

"How's it going, Perce?" I don't say anything about having overheard him just before.

He doesn't answer right away. "Did you hear about Daddy?"

My pulse starts racing. "No, what?"

"He has to have a kidney out."

That's bad, I think. "Oh?" I say carefully.

Percy looks up at me. "Do you know what kidneys do?"

I do, of course. "No. You tell me."

"They're very important. They help your body get rid of bad stuff."

I nod. "But we have two of them, right?"

Percy's face lifts a bit. "Right. So Daddy's probably going to be okay. But . . ." He gulps. "But if his other kidney doesn't work so good, he'll have to have that one out. And then . . .

then he'll be really sick. I want to see him, but Mommy says she needs me to stay home to be the man of the house."

Before I can say anything, he puts a hand on my arm. His little face is fierce. "But! He won't die. Mommy told me. He won't die . . . but he'll have to go on a machine – it's called di-al-y-sis – and that'll be terrible."

I touch his knee. "He'll be okay, Percy. You'll see."

He looks at me with brimming eyes. "Do you really think so?"

I nod. Hold out my arms. Percy leans into me. I can feel his body trembling as he struggles not to cry. He takes several deep breaths. Holding him, I pray I've told him the truth.

I stroke his hair for a moment, then leave. Even though his room probably needs it, badly, this doesn't seem like the best time to clean it.

I cross the hall and start vacuuming Gwen's room. It's pretty clean, since she hasn't been sleeping up here. Even so, I clean under the bed, in the corners, under the dresser. The entire time, memories are flashing into my mind, how we used to sit on the window seat and look out at Mount Odin and make up stories about Odin, Thor, Freya, Tyr, and all the other gods and god-desses who lived up there – in my stories they always killed each other, in Gwen's they always made up. How we used to stand in front of the mirror, pretending we were fashion models and striking runway poses.

I push those thoughts out of my mind, sweeping the vacuum over the rug. As I swing toward the doorway, the vacuum bumps the closet door open, and I see a stack of framed pictures on the floor. *That's odd,* I think. Even though I know I'm snooping, I turn off the machine and lift the first one.

It's a picture of Gwen at about seven, with little mouse ears, her hands held up in front of her like paws. Carley's next to her, grinning. The next one is of Gwen dressed like a clown with bright red circles on her cheeks and nose, her hair sprouting from a dozen ponytails all over her head. Another, much more recent, shows Gwen in a gray leotard and tights, a dusky blue cape over her shoulders. She's curved over, her back rounded, so the cape falls on either side of her like a silky blanket. I remember that dance – it's the one she made up about the fog. I went to the recital. She was terrific, so light and wispy, just like mist. I rifle through the rest. All dance pictures.

I'd noticed there was something strange and bare about the house, I realize now, putting the pictures back, I just couldn't figure out what it was.

Then it hits me. If Gwen took all these pictures down, she must really mean it about not dancing. I feel an ache in my gut.

I start up the vacuum cleaner again, and as I do, I hear that whining sound that means that something's gotten caught in the nozzle. I shut it off and lift up the head. There's a sheet of paper caught in the internal wheels. I pull it out slowly, carefully, so as not to tear it and leave a piece stuck inside. The corner's ripped, but the rest is okay.

"DANCEMAKERS," it says at the top. I scan the rest. God, it sounds perfect. Exactly what Gwen's been longing for.

I don't know if she can still go, but I feel bad that I mangled the paper. Never mind that I'm not talking to her. I go downstairs, walk over to her window spot, and hold out the sheet. "Sorry, this got chewed up by the –"

She jumps up awkwardly and snatches it out of my hand. "Where'd you get that?" Then, before I can answer, "What are you doing snooping around in my things?"

"Hey, back off! I wasn't snooping. It was in the closet. It got caught in the vacuum cleaner."

Clutching the paper to her chest, Gwen sits down, turning back toward the window.

I wait. I know she doesn't want to talk to me about it, but there's something about the way her back is slumped, so defeated and down, that hits me hard. "Can you still go?" I ask.

She twists in her chair to face me. "Look at me! Do you think I can dance on this leg? I can't even walk right."

"Yeah, I can see that, but maybe soon –"

"It's too painful. Too weak."

"Okay," I say, "but what about in a while? You give it a rest, get some treatment –"

Gwen shakes her head. "It's over."

"What, like forever? No more dancing?"

"Finished." She turns back to the window.

I study her. She sounds so sure. So final. But something doesn't feel right. I just don't know what.

"So why aren't you doing anything about it?"

She twists around again. "What do you mean?"

"Well, from what I can see, you're doing squat to get better."

"What are you talking about?"

I count on my fingers. "You don't do exercises –"

"My leg's too weak."

"You don't stretch –"

"Too painful."

"Well, hell, I don't know, heat, ice, painkillers –"

"Nothing works."

"I've been here for days and I haven't seen you try anything."

Gwen's hands form into fists. "What do you know about it? I know my body, I know if it's going to get better –"

"If you're so bummed out about it, why don't you at least try? Go to physio or something, instead of just sitting there –"

"It's no use." She scowls at me. "Besides, what do you care? It's not your problem."

Why do I care? I don't have an answer for that one. But something's bothering me. It's like she's afraid. Afraid to try to get better. But why?

I shake my head. "It's like . . . you don't *want* to get better."

Gwen rises from the chair. "That is crazy! Of course I do. I'd give –" She grabs her cane and pounds it on the floor. "Why don't you just go back to your new friends and leave me alone?"

I stand there. Feel my face get hot. In a split second, I remember sitting alone in the cop station . . . the phone not ringing . . . Nikki giving me the brush-off . . .

But then I think of Zach's smile, and Tony asking me when I'll be free, and I put my hands on my hips and say, "Okay, I will!"

"After all, they're such good friends," Gwen says sarcastically.

What's that supposed to mean? What does she know? But then I think, *Of course word got around that there were others and that they ran from the fire. So what?*

"Yeah, not like you," I snap back.

The color leaves Gwen's face. "Go to hell."

I storm out of the house. I start running. I don't know where I'm going; I just thrash around in the bush for a while, then end up in the clearing. Panting, shaking, I lean back against the cedar stump and wait for my heart to stop racing. I pace around and around the stump, first one way, then the other. As angry as I've been at Gwen, I've never said those words to her. And she's never said that to me.

Tears spring to my eyes. I dash them away. I'm not crying over her.

I turn and walk home.

THIRTEEN

The next afternoon I get a call from Cal, asking me to come down to his office at the Thor Falls police station.

Great, I think, *what now?*

I walk into town, bracing myself for bad news. The judge has reviewed my case and decided I have to stay on probation. Or pay for the damages.

But Cal's all smiles as he greets me and ushers me into his office. I've finished my community work service, he tells me, and done a good job, too. I've abided by the terms of my probation. Everything's completed fair and square. I'm through.

He shows me where he and Bridget have both already signed the form. Now all I have to do is sign it, too.

He hands me a pen. I scrawl my name. He tears off a copy and slides it across the table. "Congratulations, Molly. I'm proud of you. You're free."

For a moment, I feel oddly flat. Have I really put in thirty hours already?

But then the word registers. *Free.* I think of what Tony said. I grin as I grab my copy and stand up. I'm about to get my life back. Staying clean has been much less of a drag than I expected, but boy, am I ready to party now.

"By the way," Cal says, opening his office door and leading me out, "it looks like I owe you an apology."

"For what?"

"For not believing you when you said you were alone in the cabin."

I stop dead. "Huh?"

He pauses with his hand on the doorknob. "Your story has been corroborated. I thought you'd like to know."

"What?"

"Constable Sawchuk told me."

"Did I hear my name?" someone says from the hall.

I turn. It's Constable Sawchuk.

Motioning him over, Cal says, "I was just telling Molly what you told me."

Constable Sawchuk nods. "Right. It turns out that someone living along the trail to the Torrances' saw a bunch of teenagers running past her place the night of the fire. She called in and I checked it out. By asking around, I was able to piece together who the kids were, and I brought them in for questioning."

He brought them in? When? Why didn't I hear about this?

"They all denied having ever set foot in the cabin, or having anything to do with the fire, just like you said," Constable

Sawchuk goes on. "Apparently they'd been hanging around on the beach. When they saw the flames, they were afraid they'd be connected to the fire, so they took off." He looks down, swallows. "It looks like you really were alone that night, Molly. I . . . uh . . . apologize for doubting your word."

"Me too," Cal says, smiling at me.

I stand there, stunned. For a moment I actually feel faint, and sway a little.

"Molly? Are you okay?" Cal asks, grabbing my elbow.

I can hear the blood pounding in my ears, but I manage to say, "Uh . . . yeah . . . bye."

Stuffing the form into my pocket, I stumble out the door, down the street, automatically putting one foot in front of the other.

It's true. I can't deny it anymore. They really did shaft me. Really did hang me out to dry. And they had no intention of taking me back.

I'm furious. I feel like throwing up. I feel like a fool. I want to punch them. My face burns with humiliation. How could I have been so stupid?

This big hole opens up inside me. Who can I turn to? Who is there for me?

Not those idiots.

Not Gwen.

The hole yawns bigger, emptier.

I turn and run.

There was a knock at the kitchen door. Gwen groaned. Her mother had just left for Vancouver, where her father was scheduled to have his kidney surgery the next morning. Her mom had been a bundle of nerves, constantly misplacing her keys, her purse, her coat, as she ran through her last-minute instructions. Percy had clung to his mother as she got ready to leave, then had run upstairs in tears the minute the door closed. Gwen was desperately trying not to think about what her father was about to go through . . . and what might happen if the operation didn't go well. Dealing with whoever was at the door was the last thing she wanted to do.

She pushed herself out of the chair just as a familiar voice called from the kitchen. "Hello? Gwen, you there?"

Oh no. Susie.

Then, "Hey, Gwen."

"How's it going?"

Carley. And Janelle.

They came into the living room.

Gwen forced a smile. "Hey, guys."

"Gwen, guess what?" Susie said, giving her a hug. Before Gwen could hazard a guess, Susie went on, "Laredo's got a cappuccino machine."

"Huh?"

"Laredo's Café," Carley told her, grinning. "Just think –

cappuccino comes to Thor Falls!"

"We've hit the big time!" Janelle said, and the three girls laughed.

"So we came to get you. We've got to go check it out," Susie said.

Gwen shook her head. "I . . . I don't drink coffee."

"Hot chocolate, then. Who cares?" Susie said.

"I really don't feel like it —"

"Come on, Gwen, it'll be fun," Carley said.

"We want to try it out before the whole town hears about it," Janelle added.

"You know, I'm really tired. Maybe another time," Gwen began, but Susie had already grabbed Gwen's jacket and was thrusting it at her.

"No excuses," Susie said. "You need to get out, Gwen. It'll be a hoot. And someday you can tell your grandchildren you had the first foamed drink in Thor Falls."

When Susie stuffed Gwen's arm into the sleeve, Gwen realized she was defeated. *Well, the sooner we leave, the sooner I can get back,* she thought. Shrugging on her jacket the rest of the way, she called up the stairs, "Percy! I'm going into town. Will you be okay for half an hour?"

"Yeah," came a voice hoarse from crying.

Gwen followed her friends out of the house and climbed into Carley's mom's car.

———

I stagger and trip over a rock, falling against the cedar stump.

"Whoa," I say out loud, jerking my arm upright to keep from dropping the bottle. The vodka sloshes around, but I manage to hold the bottle up.

"Good catch," I tell myself. "That deserves a drink." I tilt up the bottle and take a good long glug. It burns as I swallow, but right now I don't mind – I even want – the pain. Booze dribbles down my chin. I wipe it off with my sleeve.

I lean against the stump for balance, feeling a knot dig into my back. Me, a bottle, and a dead cedar tree. Some party.

After running away from the police station, I'd headed for the liquor store and paid an older kid – ironically, Teresa's brother, Wayne – to buy me a bottle. Then I'd made for the clearing. Where else was there to go?

I'd been feeling pretty pleased about my sober streak – three weeks and counting – but what was the point of staying clean now? My probation was over. Besides, I needed a drink. Or three.

What I didn't expect was how hard it would hit me. Going from zero to half a mickey had definitely put me on my ass. But who cared? I deserved to feel good.

Trouble was, I didn't feel so good. I just felt blotto. Slow and thick and dizzy. And the roach I'd found in my wallet – just a few tokes left, enough for a slight buzz – had only made me feel muddier.

Well, I decide now, there's only one cure for that – have another drink. "Cheers," I say, lifting the bottle and toasting a nonexistent buddy. "Bottoms up. For whatever ails you, nails you, fails you. Oh yeah, that's a good one. Fails you." I tip the bottle up.

That thought brings back the empty hole, and if there's one thing I don't want to feel, it's that's big emptiness. I shake my head violently as if to drive out the thought, and I fall down.

"Crap," I say, dropping the bottle, watching the rest of the vodka spill onto the dirt. I push myself up. Now my hands are caked with mud. I reach into my pocket to see if there's a tissue lurking in there and feel a piece of paper. I pull it out.

It's the release form Cal gave me. Proof of time served. My liberation.

Yeah, right, I think. *Liberation to what?*

Tears sting my eyes.

I brush them away.

A thought nags at me. Just like Constable Sawchuk and Cal apologized to me, I owe Gwen an apology for accusing her of ratting me out. I never did say I was sorry. Even though I'm not talking to her, I don't like to leave that hanging.

I'll go and apologize, I decide. And *then* I won't talk to her.

I pound on the door. When no one answers, I jerk it open. "Hello? Anybody home?"

I start crossing the kitchen. The lights are off, and in the

late afternoon dusk, it's dim inside. Crash! Oops. Didn't see
that chair.

Percy comes in.

"Hey, Perce, old buddy, old pal, how's it hanging?"

"Huh?"

Smiling at his baffled expression, I peer into the living room.
It's empty. "Where's Gwen?"

"She went out with some girls."

"Who?"

He shrugs. "Didn't see. Sounded like Susie. A couple of
others."

Susie, Carley, and Janelle, I think. Gwen's new group. The
sisters of mercy. A tight little club in which I, most definitely,
am not included.

I wobble for a moment and grab the counter for balance.

Percy looks at me. "Are you . . . drunk?"

With my finger, I notch a checkmark in the air. "Smart boy!
Score one for Percy!"

He peers at me curiously, as if trying to see what "drunk"
looks like. "You smell," he says finally.

"No, no, no," I tell him. "That's the pot. Vodka doesn't smell.
That's one good thing about vodka. That, and it makes you feel
great!"

I whirl around, arms outflung. Actually, it doesn't feel so
great. I grab Percy's shoulder.

He looks up at me, his eyes wide with concern. Poor kid.

Seems like he always has that look on his face these days. Well, no wonder. His dad's wrecked, his mom's hardly home, his sister's like a shadow. I recall the last time I was here, when I overheard him arguing with Gwen. What were they arguing about? I try to remember. Oh, yeah . . .

"Hey, Percy."

"Yeah?"

"How'd you like to go up Mount Odin?"

"What, now?"

"Yeah!"

"With you?"

"Yeah. See where the avalanche was."

His eyes widen. "Do you know where?"

"No. But it can't be too hard to find, can it?"

He doesn't answer.

"Well?"

"I'm not supposed to go anywhere . . . and you're – well, you know."

I giggle, ruffling his hair. "Don't you worry about that. I'm fine."

He squirms. I can tell he really wants to go. And for some reason I really do, too. I want to do this for him. And for me. I want to see. Sort of pay tribute to Andrew. Besides, I've got nobody else to hang out with. It's me and the nine-year-old brother of my ex–best friend. How's that for a joke? Too bad it's not funny.

"You said you wanted to see the place," I say.

He sighs. "I do. I really do."

"Well then?"

"Shouldn't we wait for Gwen? She said she'd be back soon."

That's all I need, a nice visit with Gwen and the girls. I shake my head. "We'll be quick. We'll go and come back so fast I bet she'll never know we were gone."

"Okay," he says, and a smile starts. "Just let me get my jacket." He scribbles a note, just in case – "Gone for a walk with Molly" – and we're off.

FOURTEEN

By the time we get to the trail it's nearly dark. Percy asks, "Are you sure, Molly?"

"Sure, I'm sure," I say. "I mean, we've come this far, it'd be stupid to turn back. And it's not like we're going to be bashing through the woods. We're going to be on a trail, and you can't get lost on a trail, right?"

"Right."

"So there you go," I say, and we head uphill. When we get to the bridge, I'm huffing like a maniac. I haven't been up here in a while, and I've forgotten how hard the trek is.

We carry on. I have to concentrate on putting one foot in front of the other; sometimes my footsteps curve from side to side and I step off the trail into grass and brush. "Whoopsy," I say. I tell myself to think of it as a march and that'll help me go in a straight line. "Hup, two, three, four," I chant, lifting my knees. I take Percy's hand and swing it in rhythm, forward and back – "Hup, two, three, four" – and soon he's laughing too.

But his laughter dies down when we come around that last bend. He goes very still. You can hardly see anything, it's just about dark, but you can make out the black shadows of the fallen trees and the glint where boulders have been scraped and the clumps of torn-up, tangled brush and the lighter tone of the bare patches of earth against the foliage surrounding them. We're still holding hands, and I can feel him trembling. Then he throws himself into my arms and starts bawling, and then I'm bawling too, I don't even know why, and we're holding onto each other, and I feel dizzy and I don't know if it's the booze and pot or the tears, all I know is that Percy needs me right now and that feels good, really good, and I hug him, hard.

Finally he stops crying and wipes his face on his sleeve, and I do the same. He heaves a great sigh. I let him collect himself. He turns to me and says, "Okay, we can go now."

I take his hand again and start leading him down the trail.

"Uh, Molly?"

"Yeah?"

"I think it's that way."

I look. The trail he's pointing to melts into darkness. "Nuh-uh, Percy, it's this way."

"Are you sure?"

"Have I been up here a million times?" Well, not a million, exactly. Half a dozen, maybe, mostly when I was little. I don't say that.

"Yeah."

"Okay, then."

We continue. I'm straining my eyes to see. But we're going downhill so it must be right. After a while, though, the trail changes underfoot, and instead of dirt and gravel it feels like brush. I don't remember walking on this before. I stop. I slap him on the back. "You know what, Percy? You were right. We'd better turn around."

So we do. Percy's steps feel more confident now next to mine.

"I should've known that a mountain man like you would know the way, right?"

He gives a halfhearted giggle.

It's completely dark now. We leave the brush and are back on the gravel. That's good. But soon we're going uphill, and we're not supposed to be. I stop.

"Molly?" Percy's voice sounds very small.

"Yeah?"

"Are we lost?"

"Of course not!"

We carry on, side by side. We come to a fork – at least, I think it's a fork, it's hard to tell. We take the trail that seems to go downhill. But soon we're in the woods. Trees close in around us, and I know this can't be right, so we turn around and walk back the way we came.

"Molly?"

"Yeah?"

"I'm cold."

As soon as he says that I realize that I'm cold, too. Freezing, in fact. All I have on is a hoodie, and the sweat that soaked my clothes on the climb up is now drying in the chill air, and I'm shivering.

"Well, you just come here then," I say in a fake-hearty voice. I rub him up and down, his arms, his back. "There. Better?"

"A little."

We continue walking. I have no idea where we are. My head feels thick and dozy, and I feel unsteady. Percy grips my hand. He doesn't say anything. I'm feeling with my feet, trying to stay on the path; I'm trying to listen for the creek, and I can hear its rush, all right – but it seems to be everywhere, above us, below us, on either side of us. That's no help.

There's a sudden rustle in the bushes nearby, then a crack like a branch snapping. Percy and I both gasp and practically jump into each other's arms.

"What was that?" he whispers.

My mind races. It's too early for bears. And it wasn't loud enough for a bear. A coyote? A deer? Oh my god, what if it's a cougar? A shiver runs down my back at the thought of a cougar stalking us through the woods.

I fake a laugh. "Nothing," I say. "Probably just a squirrel. Or a bird."

"I'm scared," Percy says.

I grip his hand tighter, pulling him along. "Don't worry," I say, trying not to hear how shaky my own voice sounds. "We're fine –"

All of a sudden the trail isn't there. It just disappears from under my right foot. I fall down a slope, pitching awkwardly, pulling Percy with me. As we fall I hear a sickening thud and Percy yells, "Ow! My arm!" He screams as we land, sprawling, on some bushes. We haven't fallen far, just a few feet, I think, but I can't face getting up, my head is spinning and I can't bring myself to move. Percy is shrieking and I pull him onto my lap and we're both shaking and crying, and I think, *What have I done?*

Finally, Gwen thought, opening the kitchen door, *I'm home.* She'd pretended to be having fun sitting in Laredo's, sipping foamed hot chocolate from one of those bowl cups, going along with the others in pretending they were in Paris, but the whole time, she'd been wishing to be back in her chair, alone, not having to make conversation. Her friends were great, and they'd tried really hard to cheer her up – telling her about Jake Tyler's latest bonehead move; telling her that Danny had been pestering them, asking them every day how she was doing, whether she'd be coming back to school anytime soon, while they elbowed her and gave her teasing smiles. Gwen had tried to smile back. She just wasn't in the mood.

She took off her jacket and was about to flop into her chair when she suddenly felt that something wasn't quite right.

"Percy?"

No answer.

She went to the foot of the stairs. "Perce?"

Silence.

She felt a prickle of concern. Percy wasn't supposed to go anywhere without telling her. It wasn't like him to just take off. And it was nearly dark.

She went upstairs. His room was empty. She checked the coat hooks in the kitchen. His jacket was gone.

Panic started building. She moved from room to room – and then she spotted the note, propped up on the kitchen table. She'd overlooked it when she came in.

"Gone for a walk with Molly."

What? Gwen thought. At this hour? And why with Molly, of all people? Sure, she'd been aware that Molly had been cozying up to Percy lately. Molly probably thought Gwen hadn't noticed, but she had. Molly had been nosing in, acting like *she* was Percy's sister, and Gwen didn't like it one bit – even if Molly and Percy had been buddies from way back.

But why would Percy go for a walk with Molly? And where would they go?

Then it came to her.

No.

But she knew that must be it. Knew it in her bones. He must have talked her into it.

A shudder shivered through her.

I can't go up there. I can't.

But she had to. There was no way of knowing how long

they'd been gone. Gwen had taken a lot longer than the half
hour she'd promised. It was just about dark. They should have
been back by now. What if –

No! No time for that. She threw on a jacket, grabbed a flashlight and her cane, and half-hobbled, half-ran out the door.

The flashlight beam illuminated only a small circle of the trail,
creating a moving spotlight as Gwen swung it back and forth,
lighting up treetops and the path and the creek and the brush,
calling, "Percy! Percy?"

Nothing, just the sound of the falls, her own ragged breathing in her ears.

She didn't let herself think. She talked herself over the bridge,
over the water's roar. *I can do this, it's okay, I just need to find
them, I can do this . . .*

Around the next switchback.

"Percy! Molly! Percy!"

She stopped. Was that a faint sound, a voice? "Percy?"

No.

Onward.

The next switchback. The next. The higher she climbed, the
harder it was to put one foot in front of another. Knowing what
lay ahead.

Don't think! Don't remember, she told herself.

She walked on, her footsteps slowing, her heart pounding.

"Percy!"

No answer.

She came around a bend, swung the flashlight back and forth. On one side of the trail the beam lit up standing trees that reached toward the sky; on the other, it shone on nothing but fallen trees, their roots sticking up in the air. Broken trunks, torn-up brush, gouged earth.

Gwen froze. Her breathing became shallow. She felt light-headed. Sweat ran down under each armpit.

No! I can't, I can't, I can't –

Percy needs you, she told herself. *You've got to –*

She couldn't move. She stood there, shaking. She closed her eyes, tried to block her ears, but it all came back: the wind . . . the roar . . . the fury of the cascading snow . . . her father's body tossed helplessly down the slope . . .

With a cry, Gwen sank to the ground, the cane and flashlight falling from her hands. She screamed . . . and screamed . . .

I lift my head. What's that?

"Percy, did you hear –"

His head jerks up too. He goes still, listening.

It's faint. It sounds like –

"What –"

"Sh!"

It sounds like someone screaming, high-pitched and shrill. But is it a person? A gray owl's cry can sound like a woman screaming,

I remember Andrew telling me. But this repeats, over and over.

"It's Gwen!" Percy says.

I think so too. It must be. She must be searching for us, calling for us. I hope so. I hope not.

I'm cold and wet, my legs are asleep, my back aches, my head feels like mud, I feel sick to my stomach. I push Percy up into a standing position. He gives a cry as his arm jerks. I force myself to stand. I sway. Then I grab Percy's good hand and we stumble downhill, in the direction of the cries.

Half the time I don't know if we're even on the trail or stumbling through the brush at the side of it. Percy whimpers, sometimes yelping as his arm bangs against his side. I have no idea where we're going; we're just following the sound, as if it's a foghorn guiding us home.

We get closer to the screaming. "Gwen!" Percy yells, though she's still out of sight.

Closer. Louder. It's definitely Gwen, I can tell. But as we draw nearer, I realize that she's not calling out our names, she's just screaming wordless cries. Why?

We come around a bend. She's on her knees, right beside the avalanche scar, rocking back and forth, hands over her face. Her screams pierce the night. A flashlight lies on the trail beside her, its beam lighting the roots of a fallen tree.

Percy lets go of my hand. He launches himself at Gwen, curling over her back, wrapping his good arm around her.

"Gwen!"

That seems to snap her out of it. She jerks her head up, and the screams die abruptly.

"Percy! Oh my God, Percy!"

She turns and gathers him into her arms. They sit there, clinging to one another.

"Gwen! My arm!" He begins to weep, shaking, and Gwen crushes him to her chest, weeping herself, crooning, "Percy, Percy, it's okay, I've got you, it's okay . . ."

I pick up the flashlight, then Gwen's cane, which is lying nearby.

She looks up at me. "You idiot. You nearly got my brother killed!"

I don't say anything.

Gwen stands, lifting Percy to his feet. "You're crazy! Do you realize what you —"

"Gwen! I want to go home!" Percy wails.

Holding Percy close, Gwen glares over his head at me with such a look of hatred that I can see it even in the dark.

"Okay, Perce," she says, and I can tell she's struggling to speak calmly. "Let's go home."

I hand her the flashlight. She turns away and starts down the hill, her arm around Percy's good shoulder.

I follow with the cane.

FIFTEEN

Gwen's upstairs a long time. I hear her murmuring to Percy, the sound of running water, his voice, high and boyish, more murmurs. Then, gradually, silence.

I'm sitting on the living room floor, my knees drawn to my chest, still in my wet, dirty clothes. I know I should leave. Go home. Disappear. But I can't bring myself to move. I'm not even drunk anymore, it's not that. In fact, I feel almost too clear-headed. Clearheaded enough to know what I've done, and to feel terrible about it.

Gwen comes downstairs. A look of surprise, then anger, crosses her face. "What are you still doing here? Why don't you get the hell out?" As she moves across the room, I notice that her limp is more pronounced than it's been lately. She's gripping the cane tightly.

I have no answer for that. Instead I say, "Percy's arm . . . ?"

"Not broken – no thanks to you."

I heave a sigh.

"What the hell were you doing?"

"I –"

"You nearly got my brother killed, you realize that?"

"No, I –"

"Taking him up on the mountain – after dark – stumbling drunk! You're crazy. You're a maniac."

I curl over my knees. "I didn't mean to . . ."

"Who gives a damn what you meant? You got him lost! What were you doing with him, anyway?"

"Trying to make him feel better."

"Feel better?"

I look up. "He wanted to go. He asked you, but you said no –" I stop abruptly.

Gwen takes a step closer. "How do you know that?"

My cheeks grow warm. "I . . . heard you . . . heard the two of you arguing . . ."

Gwen glares at me. "You sneak! How dare you eavesdrop on us!"

"I didn't mean to. I was just there."

"It's none of your business!"

I know she's right. I know I'm wrong. But then I think of Percy's voice when he pleaded with her, his face when I said I'd take him. "At least I paid attention to him. Which is more than you did."

"What do you mean?"

"I've been around. I see. You've been too busy sitting in your chair, feeling sorry for yourself."

"That's not true."

"It is so. That's why Percy turned to me. It was all about your dad."

"My dad?" Gwen looks startled. Her face goes pale. "What are you trying to say?"

"Percy wanted to see where it happened, so he could feel closer to your dad. Because he misses him. And worries about him."

As I say these words, I realize something. In all the time I've been around since the fire, I haven't once heard Gwen mention her dad. Talk to him on the phone. Ask a question about him.

I add, "Which is more than I can say for you."

"What?"

"I thought you cared about him."

"I do!"

"Loved him."

"I do."

"Well, you're sure not acting like it. For God's sake, Gwen, he's suffering."

"I know!" A wail.

"For all you know, he could be dying in Vancouver –"

I'm not prepared for Gwen's reaction. She jerks as if she's been shot. A look of terror comes over her face. "Don't say that!" she screams. Then again, quieter, pleading, her voice breaking, "Don't say that."

My mind starts jumping around. Gwen's dad. His injuries. Her injury. Gwen on the mountain, kneeling at the avalanche site, screaming. The way she's gripping the cane. This terrified look on her face.

Somehow I know there's more to this. I don't know what. It's not even a clear thought, just a feeling, a *knowing*, in my gut.

I jump to my feet, seize Gwen by the arm. "Something happened up there, Gwen. What was it?"

Dropping the cane, she covers her eyes. "I can't," she says into her hands.

"Tell me!" I shout. Then, more gently, "Tell me what happened, Gwen."

"No . . ."

"Gwen."

"Oh God, oh God –" She doubles over, clutching her middle, then sinks to her knees, just like on the mountain. "It's all my fault!"

"What, Gwen?"

"I made him get hurt. It was me!"

"What was you?"

"My dad – the avalanche – oh God –" She leans back into a sitting position, pulls in her knees, wraps her arms around them.

I kneel beside her. "Tell me."

She shakes her head. "It's too terrible."

"Tell me."

She searches my face as if she's looking for something. Then, as if she's found it, she starts speaking.

"We had a big fight. . . . I – I wanted to go to Dancemakers
– oh, I wanted it so bad –"

She hunches her shoulders and sobs onto her knees.

I wait.

"But my dad said no . . . and I shouted at him . . . and he
said we should go down . . . but I wouldn't – I was so mad, I
wouldn't listen – and then . . . then . . . the avalanche came –"

She sits up, putting her hands over her face. "Oh God, it was
so terrifying, the noise and wind, this wall of snow – and he
said, 'Gwen, ski!' – he wanted to save me!" She gives a cry.

"And the snow swept me away . . . and the last thing I saw
was my dad's body thrown down the mountain and buried."

She wails, holding herself. "And he got hurt so bad . . . and
he might never get better . . . and it's all my fault!"

"Gwen –"

"And I hardly got hurt at all!" She strikes her leg as if trying
to inflict more pain.

"Gwen, stop it."

"It's so unfair –"

"Gwen –"

"I can never make up for it. Never!"

I don't know what to do to get her to stop, so I do the first
thing that comes to mind. Grab her shoulders and shake her.
"Shut up!"

She looks at me, stunned.

"It wasn't your fault."

"It was."

"No –"

She shakes her head. "I don't care what you say, I know what I did."

"*You* didn't cause the avalanche!"

"But I wouldn't come down."

"So? Would it have made any difference? If you came down when your dad said you should, would you still have got caught in it?"

A pause. I watch her eyes flick back and forth, as if she's replaying the scene, calculating. "Yes."

"See?"

"But – but it's not fair that he got hurt so bad and I didn't."

"Yeah. It's not."

Gwen nods. "That's why I –"

"You're not God. It's not *your* fault your dad got it worse. Things happen."

Gwen's eyes fill with tears. "But if I hadn't –"

"Enough already. Stop blaming yourself for something you didn't do."

This look comes over her face. A lightening. A lifting. It's as if I can see inside her head. I can see her mind go toward that thought, then skitter away, afraid to trust it.

"There's only one way to get over this, Gwen," I say.

"What?"

"Talk to your dad."

A pause. "I can't."

"You've got to."

"But he's – he's not well enough."

"No excuses, Gwen."

"But – but what if he won't talk to me?" Then, softer, "What if he doesn't forgive me?"

"He will."

I can feel her holding her breath. "Do you really think so?" It's a whisper.

I nod.

Her face cracks. It melts. Then, without warning, she throws her arms around me and starts sobbing. These are sobs from deep in the belly, wracking, grunting cries. She clings to me, and I cling to her, and then I'm crying too. I'm bawling, pressing my face into her skinny, frail shoulder.

"Oh, Molly . . . Molly . . ." she gasps.

She cries, her slender body shaking until, gradually, her sobs lessen and hush and finally stop. Heaving a sigh, she pushes herself away. Her eyes are red, her nose is running, tears cling to her lashes, but she gives me a tremulous smile.

"Molly?"

"Yeah?"

"Thanks."

Embarrassed, I wave a hand. "I didn't –"

"No. Really. Thanks."

I stand. Put out my hand and pull Gwen up. I can see that there's a lightness, albeit a tired one, about her – and I'm happy for her, really I am, and I'm glad I helped. But at the same time, I feel funny. Now what? Where do I stand? Are we friends again? Or will we go back to the way it was? And what then? What if Gwen turns away again? Who do I have?

I feel that yawning hole again. The emptiness.

I put my hands in my pockets and feel a paper there. I pull it out. It's the form from Cal.

I'm free, I think bitterly.

"What's that?" Gwen asks.

"My release form. Saying I've served my probation. Finished my community service work. I'm through here."

Yeah, I'm free all right. I shove the paper back in my pocket.

Gwen's face hardens. "So go," she says harshly. "I'm not keeping you."

"What?"

"Go," Gwen says again. "You've done your time. You have the paper to prove it."

"Gwen –"

"You don't want to be here, Molly. So just go back to your new friends!"

I jerk.

"They're waiting for you to *have fun*, right? And I'm no fun, remember?"

She glares at me. I turn and run out of the house. But once on the porch, I can't go any farther. I collapse on a chair and bury my face in my hands.

Gwen sank into a living room chair, heartbroken. She had thought that she and Molly were pulling back together. Molly had reached out to her, and Gwen had confessed her darkest secret and cried on Molly's shoulder. And now, all Molly cared about was that she was finished with her community service work and didn't have to stick around any longer.

Tears stung Gwen's eyes. *Stupid*, she scolded herself, *to let this hurt all over again.*

Wiping her eyes, she heard something. Percy? No, quiet upstairs. Seemed to be outside.

She listened. A bird? An animal crying out?

She crossed to the kitchen door and opened it. A shape huddled in the dim light.

"Molly!"

She was curled on a chair, arms wrapped around her legs, sobbing.

Gwen reached out a hand. "Molly, what – "

Molly pulled deeper into herself.

"Molly, what is it? What's the matter?"

Molly jerked away. Deep wrenching cries came from her.

"Molly, please… I'm sorry I said that about your friends."

A wail. "I. . .have. . .no. . .friends."

Gwen hesitated. Then she lowered herself onto the chair, squeezing beside Molly. She put her arms around her. She didn't say anything, just held Molly as she cried.

Finally Molly began to speak. She told Gwen about how much fun she'd been having, how she'd thought she was part of the group, how she'd felt even more in the thick of things when she'd found them a place to party.

"Oh, Gwen, I'm so sorry about the cabin!" she said, weeping again.

Gwen waited.

"When the fire started, I was so panicked, I didn't know what to do. We just had to save the cabin – I couldn't let it burn down! – but it spread so fast . . . and they didn't do anything. They were so freaked out. . . . They batted out a few sparks, but then they just took off." Molly sniffled. "I was so hurt. I mean, they left me there in the flames! But at the same time, I couldn't blame them. It *was* terrifying. I was freaked out too."

After her arrest, Molly explained, she kept waiting for the others to come forward and share the blame.

"No one did," she said in a heavy voice. "No one even called to say they were sorry or see how I was." She dashed tears from her eyes. "But I told myself they were just afraid. I mean, Tony had been busted before, and Zach had been picked up for underage drinking, so they couldn't risk getting in trouble again. I told myself they were just lying low, that as soon as my probation was over they'd all come back, and it would be just like before." Tears filled her eyes. "But today . . ." Her lip trembled. "Today . . ."

"What, Molly?" Gwen touched her shoulder. "What happened?"

Tears rolled down Molly's cheeks as she told Gwen what Constable Sawchuk had said. "They never cared about me, Gwen! They were never really my friends. I was just someone to party with . . . someone to find them a free place to get drunk in . . . and then . . . forget about." She put her hands over her face. "Oh, Gwen, how could I have been so stupid?"

Gwen stroked her shoulder. "You're not stupid."

"I am!" Molly moaned. "And now . . . now . . ." She pulled her legs up into a tuck position, lowered her head to her knees, and sobbed, " I have no one."

Gwen waited until Molly's cries were stilled. For a brief moment, she thought about what her other friends would say. Carley and Susie and Janelle would think she'd gone off her rocker, hooking up with Molly again. But she didn't care. They all used to be friends. Maybe they could be again. In the meantime, it didn't matter. Molly was back. That was what mattered now.

"Molly," she said softly, "you have me."

SIXTEEN

"Hey." Molly nudged Gwen. "We're here."

Gwen turned with a start, looking out the bus window. She saw a parking lot full of buses, a huge stone terminal, and warehouses across the street.

"C'mon," Molly said, pulling Gwen's sleeve, "we get off here."

As if in a dream, Gwen followed her off the bus. That was how she had been all the way down the coast, in some kind of unreal, numb, this-isn't-me-and-I'm-not-really-doing-this state.

Her mother didn't know she was here. Bridget was actually on her way home. Gwen had left a long explanatory note and arranged for Percy to stay with Sally. She knew her mother wouldn't be happy.

But it wasn't her mother she was worried about — it was her father. All during the ride, she'd run through scenarios. He'd be near death, too weak to see her, and she'd never get a chance to talk to him. He'd be angry. He'd be having another operation. He'd refuse to see her.

In the bus depot, Molly asked directions. They caught a city bus south, then transferred to another going west. Storefronts and low-rise apartments gave way to classy old houses, a shopping district, city hall. Then – the tower of Vancouver General.

Gwen stopped at the entrance, leaning on her cane. Her leg throbbed. *I can't, I can't, I can't –*

"Come on," Molly said, taking her free arm. Then, more gently, "It'll be all right."

Gwen followed her inside. Lobby. Reception desk. Phones ringing. People. Lots of them. Even at night. People in wheelchairs. People clutching bouquets of flowers, magazines, fluffy stuffed animals. Over the PA a voice said, "Doctor Robinson, call 1-2-4. Doctor Robinson."

Molly guided her down the hallway, past reception, the nurse looking curiously after them but too busy to do anything about it. Past X-ray. Pediatrics. Ultrasound.

Then – Intensive Care Unit.

Gwen stopped, her mouth dry.

"Can I help you?" asked a nurse. She sat at a desk; behind her, double glass doors marked the entrance to the ward.

"Andrew Torrance," Gwen managed to say.

The nurse shook her head.

"This is his daughter," Molly asserted.

"Gwen?"

Gwen nodded.

The nurse smiled. "He's told me about you."

Gwen's mouth was too dry to smile. *What did he say?*

"Can she see him?" Molly asked.

"He's not here anymore," the nurse said.

"Where is he?"

"Moved to a surgical unit a couple of days ago," the nurse said. "He had renal surgery – yesterday, I believe. Should be out of post-op by now."

Oh God, was that good or bad?

Down the hall, up another elevator, down another hall. Trolleys of empty food trays. Patients pushing IV stands. "Doctor Sharpe to Emergency. Doctor Sharpe," said a voice over the PA.

Another nursing station. Molly spoke to the nurse.

"Are you family?" the nurse asked.

"I am," Gwen replied.

"Only family allowed," the nurse said to Molly. "You'll have to wait here."

Gwen turned her terror-filled eyes toward Molly.

"Go on," Molly said softly, "you'll be fine. I'll be right here."

Gwen turned, limped down the hall to the room the nurse had pointed out. The door was slightly ajar. She took a deep breath and pushed it open all the way.

He was sleeping, propped up on pillows. Green hospital gown, IV drip in his arm, head lolling to the side. His beard was longer, his face thinner – no, not just his face, his whole body, like a shrunken version of his old self. Even in sleep, his face looked more lined.

His eyes opened. Stared a moment. "Gwen!" Raspy, hoarse.

"Daddy!"

He held out his arms. She rushed in. The cane fell to the floor.

"Dad –" She burst into tears.

"Gwennie, my sweet girl, you're okay, you're okay. I'm sorry, I'm so terribly sorry –" Tears slid down his cheeks.

Choking off a cry, Gwen lifted her head. "What?"

He paused a moment, regaining control, then seemed to make an effort to speak. "For letting you get hurt. If you only knew what I've been going through, worrying about you –"

"Worrying about *me?* But Dad, it was *my* fault."

"What do you mean?"

Gwen forced herself to look in his eyes. "For arguing. For refusing to go down. For making us stay up there too late –"

The flood burst. She lay her head down on his chest and sobbed.

"Oh, Gwen, is that what you've been thinking?"

She nodded against his chest.

"Gwen, you're wrong, completely wrong. It was my fault."

Gwen began, "But –"

"No," he said sharply.

She lifted her head.

"Now, you listen to me, Gwen. You're a kid, I'm an adult. I was responsible. I should have known better. God, I *did* know better, that's the hell of it. I knew, when we were talking to

Simon, even before then, when the weather changed, that it wasn't safe, that we should get down. When my skis were sticking – remember? – I knew the conditions were changing. But I didn't want to, I was having too much fun –"

"But I argued. I skied away –"

"It was too late long before that. And I knew it." His voice cracked. "When Mom told me you hurt your leg, you couldn't dance, you were depressed –"

"But you were hurt so bad."

"Lucky to be alive."

"Daddy, I'm so sorry." She started crying again.

"Gwen, have you been blaming yourself this whole time?"

She nodded.

"Oh, honey, what you've gone through! Listen. We didn't get caught because of that argument. We got caught because I was a fool, and because we had bad luck. That's all. Do you hear me?"

She looked at him. Hesitantly, she nodded again.

He took her hands. "Gwen, will you forgive me?"

"Oh, Dad!" Arms around each other, they cried, then finally dried their eyes and sat looking at each other.

Gwen put a hand on his arm. "What about you? Will you be okay?"

He sighed. "It's been rough, I won't deny it, and it's going to take a long time to get my strength back. But yes, I think so. My other kidney seems to be okay, and my collapsed lung is better, and I seem to be fine without my spleen. Won't be doing any telemarking for a while, though."

Gwen managed a smile.

"What about your leg?" he asked.

She shrugged. "It hurts."

"What is it?"

"I don't know. They can't find anything wrong." When he didn't answer, she added, "They think it's all in my head."

"Mom says you're talking about quitting dancing. She says you've just given up."

"What's the use –"

"Now, you listen to me, Gwen. I don't want to hear that. How can you even think that way? You, not dancing?"

"But I can't –"

"Gwen, you've got to try to get better!"

"But how –"

"We'll figure it out. If it takes physiotherapy, you'll get physiotherapy. If it takes surgery, you'll get surgery. Whatever it takes."

He lifted her chin, forced her to look in his eyes. "Promise me, Gwen. Promise me you won't give up."

A wild flare of hope pulsed through her. *Could* she heal? *Could* she come back?

"Okay."

"You promise?"

A smile. "I promise."

SEVENTEEN

Gwen and Molly turned the curve past the Thor Falls bridge, and Gwen wondered, for the tenth time, what on earth Molly was up to. And where Molly had been for the last week, and why she'd suddenly popped up today.

After they'd returned from Vancouver, they'd hung out non-stop, rediscovering each other. They'd talked the whole way back to Norse River, heads together in the gray bus seats, and kept right on going once they'd come home. They'd laughed. They'd cried. They'd revealed secrets and hurts. They'd found themselves finishing each other's sentences.

After a few days, Molly had abruptly disappeared. No calls, no visits, no e-mails. Nothing. Gwen had wondered what was going on. Was Molly pulling away again?

Then Molly had showed up at the house this morning, handed Gwen her shoes, and said, "Come on, we're going for a hike up Mount Odin."

Gwen had looked at her in disbelief. "No, we're not."

"Yes, we are. Come on, Gwen. I promise, it'll be worth it. Trust me."

It wasn't the promise that Gwen had trusted, it was Molly's body language. Her eyes were twinkling and her mouth was twitching and her body was quivering with excitement. It was the old Molly, with some devilment up her sleeve. So Gwen had let herself be persuaded.

It had been scary approaching Thor Falls. Not as bad as last time, not even close. Still, she'd broken into a sweat as they neared the base of the trail. Nearly turned back. But Molly took her hand and told her to just keep breathing, it was going to be okay, and, to her amazement, it was. Breathe in, breathe out, one foot in front of the other, gripping Molly's hand, and then they were over the bridge, and Gwen could let go.

It was one of those rare sunny early spring days, sunlight sparkling on the water, last night's raindrops glistening on the trees. Gwen stopped and sniffed, taking in the musty smell of last winter's leaf mold, the fresh ferny scent of this year's horsetails. Felt the sunlight on her face. Heard the chatter of a squirrel, the thrumming of a woodpecker. It felt good, after so many weeks of hiding. Of being half-alive.

They stopped hiking after a steep switchback, leaning over, hands on knees, catching their breath. After a minute, Gwen straightened up. Molly stood there, gazing out at the horizon.

"Are we stopping here?" Gwen asked.

"A little farther."

"Where will the Mystery Walk end, may I ask, oh, wise one?"

"I'll let you know. Keep walking."

Gwen smiled to herself, then walked on. She wasn't using the cane anymore. She still felt the odd twinge, but mostly her leg was all right. She couldn't understand it. She *knew* she hadn't imagined that pain – she could remember how it shot up her leg – and still did, sometimes. Yet she also knew she'd somehow invented it. And now, it seemed, she didn't need it anymore, so it was going away.

Mysterious, she thought. But it didn't matter. Her leg felt better every day.

She didn't know if it was too late to put together a dance for Dancemakers – although the deadline hadn't yet passed, she'd lost precious weeks of honing her dance. But Dancemakers didn't seem so urgent now. She could dance. She had her life to dance.

I huff along behind Gwen. It's good to be up here. Better than last time, that's for sure. I just helped Gwen conquer the bridge. Felt good. To be trusted. To see her do it.

Things are still a little strange. Mostly it feels okay. We've fallen into the old rhythms, like remembering an old tune you haven't sung in a long time. We'll be joking and laughing about all kinds of stuff – our parents, our teachers, how annoying my sisters are, how Gwen secretly loves playing Orcs and Elves with Percy, how she doesn't have a clue that Danny has the hots for her even though it's obvious to everybody else in the entire school – then one of us'll say something about a party, having fun, getting crazy, and an awkward silence falls. I'm still wondering if Gwen disapproves of me, and I guess she's still wondering if I think she's a bore. We've got a lot of talking to do. A lot of figuring out who we are. But we're here. That's good enough for now.

They hiked on. Came around a bend – and there it was. The site of the avalanche. Fallen trees, their roots sticking up in the air. Broken trunks, uprooted bushes, overturned rocks. Bare patches where the earth was scoured away like the tender skin beneath a scab. So raw, so real, in the daylight.

Gwen's heart started to race and she felt cold. She heard the roar of the sliding snow, saw the wall coming down, remembered that night, when she'd frozen, right here, unable to move –

She turned away from the mountainside, squeezing her eyes shut.

Then she felt arms around her. Gwen clung to the strength in Molly's arms, to the warmth of her support. Then she let go and forced herself to turn around. To gaze at the devastation. To face it, stare it down.

It wasn't easy. Her heart pounded. Her pulse raced. The slope was brutal and ugly and bare.

But she looked. She stood her ground. And she found that she could breathe normally. That she didn't have to crumple.

The avalanche was a scar on the land, and it was still a scar on her. But it didn't have to be one forever. She took one last look, and then they walked on.

Around a switchback. Another. Then Molly said, "Here."

Gwen stopped, turned to face her friend. A look of excitement, almost nervousness, was on Molly's face, but she wasn't saying a word. Gwen looked around, trying to figure out what it was about this spot that deserved stopping for. They were far enough away from the falls that the roar was just a steady hiss. The part of the ridge they were standing on gave a broad view of the beach below and the ocean beyond. Aside from the whisper of Thor Falls, all was quiet.

Gwen turned to Molly. "All right, you've brought me all the way up here. Now what?"

Molly reached into her backpack and handed her an iPod and portable speakers. "Press *play.*" Smile twitching.

Giving Molly a quizzical look, Gwen did. At first, nothing. Then, a hushing sound. Familiar. Whsshh . . . whsshh – waves. Waves breaking on the beach. The squawk of a gull. Then the roar of Thor Falls, up close, loud, pounding, crashing. Then the cry of an eagle, far away.

"What . . . how . . . ?"

A grin. "I taped it."

"So that's what –"

"Sh!"

Gwen quieted. More sounds – birds, the distant hoot of a ferry's horn. Snippets of music. A drumbeat. A bass line. A saxophone riff.

Then – a voice. Molly's voice. Singing. No words, just a melody, rising and falling. At times scared and small, at others defiant and strong. Singing the mountain. Singing the snow, the avalanche. Singing the terror. Singing the sound of the ocean. The sound of Thor Falls.

Molly had made this. Molly had sung for her.

Her voice rang out above the waves, above the waterfall.

Singing the dance.

Gwen looked at her friend. Molly, smiling, nodded as if to say, *Go ahead.*

Gwen turned toward the ocean. Stood a moment, scanning the horizon, watching the spots of brilliance where sunlight danced off waves.

Molly's voice soared.

Gwen raised her arms and began to dance.

ACKNOWLEDGMENTS

The author would like to thank James and Lynn Hill, Corinne and Dave Roth, Carol and John Gives, Richard Banner and Bruce Horn, Sandy Stevenson, Bruce Cookson, Ruth Nyman, Sandra Diersch, and Kathy Lowinger.